# THE
# ESSENE
# CONSPIRACY

### A NOVEL

## S. ERIC WACHTEL

THE ESSENE CONSPIRACY

Library of Congress Control Number: 2010918244

ISBN 978-0-615-42646-4

Cover design by Kimberly Martin

Dedicated to my extraordinary mother, Rose.
Her spirit and inspiration lives on.

# ACKNOWLEDGEMENTS

This book would never have become a reality without the support and encouragement of two special people in my life. First, my wife, Lynn—talented painter, gourmet chef, and writer. And my daughter, Sarah—a classic combination of intellect and beauty. I'm grateful to you both.

# AUTHORS NOTE

Although the modern State of Israel was established in 1948, Jerusalem remained a divided city until June 10, 1967. On the third day of the Six-Day War, Israeli paratroopers reclaimed the Temple Mount and raised the Israeli flag above the Dome of the Rock. Soon after, the chief chaplain of the Israeli army, Rabbi Shlomo Goren, standing with Israeli troops at the Western Wall (Wailing Wall), proclaimed, "We have taken the city of God. We are entering the Messianic era for the Jewish people, and I promise to the Christian world that what we are responsible for, we will take care of."

On June 17, 1967, as a conciliatory gesture, Israeli Defense minister Moshe Dayan ordered the removal of the Israeli flag flying above the Dome of the Rock, the immediate return of the Temple Mount to the Supreme Muslim Council—the (Jordanian) Waqf, and banned Jews from praying on the Temple Mount.

To date, Israeli policy regarding the Temple Mount remains unchanged.

# PROLOGUE

**Jerusalem, March 5, 1991**
**7:15 a.m.**

The mild morning air hinted at the promise of a brilliant spring as Israeli Finance Minister Uzi Kopelman walked briskly along an ancient narrow corridor of the Jewish Quarter leading to the Zion Gate.

Earlier that morning, in remembrance of his father who was killed, three years to the date, by a powerful bomb a Muslim terrorist had detonated in a crowded Tel Aviv restaurant, he had prayed at the Western Wall.

On his way to an emergency meeting with the director of Israeli Intelligence, his thoughts dwelled on the alarming magnitude of the financial transactions he had uncovered a day earlier.

Moments after passing an alleyway, Kopelman felt a subtle sting on the back of his neck. Instinctively raising his open right hand, the former captain of the Israeli Army soccer team swatted his neck and continued walking.

Less than a minute later, his limbs suddenly gripped by muscle paralysis, he staggered and fell to the stone pavement. Unable to move his body, he stared up in terror at the masked figure garbed in an Arab caftan looming above him. Knowing he couldn't defend himself, his heart sank.

Brandishing a dagger, the figure glared at Kopelman and said, taunting him, "You think you can stop us—you're wrong. Let this be a lesson to those who would challenge the will of God."

His energy drained, gasping for breath, Kopelman murmured in a low voice, "Please . . . I mean you no harm. Don't—"

But it was too late. Intent on fulfilling his mission, the assassin raised his dagger and plunged it deep into Uzi Kopelman's chest.

# CHAPTER 1

I t had been a long day for Harry A. McClure. At 12:20 a.m., after a late evening dinner with the chairman of a Japanese electronics manufacturer, his mind and body craved sleep. Returning to the midtown brownstone which served as both his company's offices and New York residence, he placed his right index finger against a sensor pad inconspicuously mounted to the right side of the front door. Moments after the stately door silently closed behind him, an elevator whisked him to the top floor where, unexpectedly, the distinctive ringing of his private phone shattered the serenity of the night.

The president of an international security-consulting firm, McClure surmised the late-night caller was more than likely one of a select group of clients who paid a substantial retainer for his services. Dashing down the hall to his study, he reached for the red phone on his desk and answered in a subdued tone.

"Hello?"

"Harry . . . is that you?" the caller demanded.

McClure recognized the distinctive "Texas twang" of Saunders McGee, Chairman of Bethlehem Oil, and eased into his desk chair.

"Good evening, Saunders. Do you have any idea what time it is?"

"Sorry to call so late, but I've been trying to reach you for hours. We've got a big problem in Sudan. In retaliation of our government's recent decision to list it as a state sponsor of terrorism, the Premier, Omar al-Bashir, is encouraging the Janjaweed militia to attack American operations in Sudan."

On assignment for Bethlehem Oil McClure had traveled to Sudan several times in the past two years and was familiar with Bethlehem's sizeable holdings there. Loosening his tie, he pressed the phone to his ear.

"How can I help you, Saunders?"

"We've got to get our engineering and geological team out of Sudan ASAP. I know you have friends in the Sudanese government, so I'd like you to head the team which is preparing, as we speak, to fly to there. Whatever it takes . . . I want them back on American soil alive."

"How much time do we have?"

"Not much. You've got to be in and out of the Sudan by 11 tonight."

Taking a deep breath, McClure shot back, "You realize there won't be any time to deal with unforeseen problems?"

"Yes, I understand, but we don't have a choice. Our geological exploration team in Sudan unexpectedly discovered a substantial deposit of uranium-238. If we don't act quickly, their survey maps might end up in the wrong hands."

McClure thought for a moment. "If I'm not mistaken, uranium-238 can be converted into plutonium, which then can be used to make a nuclear bomb?"

"Yes, and I don't want that to happen."

McClure shook his head and smiled to himself. *So that's it.*

McGee pressed. "Can I count on you, Harry?"

Propping himself up in his desk chair, McClure replied smugly, "Have I ever let you down?"

Gratified, McGee continued. "A car will pick you up at your brownstone in three hours and take you to Teterboro Airport where our Gulfstream is being readied for flight. My assistant, Carl Anderson, will be at the airport to fill you in on the details. Good luck, Harry!"


The Bethlehem Oil Gulfstream landed without incident in Khartoum. Met by a bribed high-ranking Sudanese government minister, the aircraft quickly refueled and taxied to a holding area alongside of the main runway. At 11:31 p.m., making final preparations for departure, McClure carefully checked the employee roster. Everyone was accounted for except Bart Rollins, the chief geologist.

The previous day, Rollins had traveled to an area in northern Sudan, close to the Libyan border, to verify the discovery of the uranium-238 reserve.

He knew from an associate with whom he had been in radio contact earlier in the day that a special plane had been dispatched to evacuate Bethlehem Oil employees from Sudan.

"Bart," the associate had warned, "you must be at the airport no later than 11 p.m. or you'll miss the plane and be stranded in Sudan." Rollins, known for being punctual, was now more than 35 minutes late. Growing anxious, McClure paced in the cockpit. Checking his watch again, he turned to the pilot. "It's 11:36. We'll give him until 11:45, but that's it."

The pilot, an Air Force veteran who had served in Vietnam, stared at McClure incredulously.

"Mr. McClure, we've already cut our chances of getting out of here damn close."

Fixing his eyes on the pilot, McClure responded, "Get the plane ready for immediate takeoff."

Nodding, a slight smile on his face, the pilot said, "Okay, we'll be ready."

At 11:45 p.m., McClure ordered the aircraft door closed. Just as he was about to signal the pilot to take off, a female voice cried out, "I think I see him." Jan Fleming, a geologist who worked for Rollins, had spotted the headlights of an approaching vehicle flashing in the distance.

Peering through another window, McClure raised the night vision binoculars suspended from his neck and focused on the flashing lights. Was this a signal or a trap? Making a split-second decision, he decided to wait a few additional minutes.

As the vehicle came within 500 feet of the aircraft, he recognized the distinctive "BO" markings on the hood of the Land Rover and the tricolor pennant flapping on the radio antennae. A cracked windshield and bullet holes in its side panels confirmed the vehicle had been fired on.

A moment after the Land Rover screeched to a halt five feet from the aircraft door, Rollins, a travel bag dangling from his shoulder, leaped from the vehicle and sprinted onto the aircraft. Quickly, the crew sealed the aircraft door.

"Let's get the hell out of here," McClure barked to the pilot through the open cockpit door.

A loud explosion lit the night sky as the Gulfstream, filled with Bethlehem Oil Company employees, taxied down the runway, majestically raised itself into the air, and headed for Nairobi, Kenya. The time on McClure's watch read 11:51 p.m.

Nine minutes later, hundreds of Janjaweed militia overran the last Bethlehem Oil Company facility two miles from Khartoum.

# CHAPTER 2

M cClure's Irish-Scottish lineage endowed him with a strong physical presence, defined angular face, magnetic blue eyes, dark brown wavy hair tinged with streaks of silver, and a deep commanding voice. Along the lower edge of his square jaw was a faint one-inch horizontal scar—the only physical reminder of a near fatal accident.

As a midshipman at the United States Naval Academy, McClure was a star lacrosse player. Now, at the age of forty-five, he kept his 6'2" body toned by rigorously working out several times a week in a specially outfitted gym tucked into the basement of his Manhattan brownstone.

Exhausted and experiencing the effects of jet lag, he slept soundly until the sensation of a warm tongue licking his outstretched hand awakened him. Sitting up, he swung his legs over the side of the bed and affectionately petted his dog,

Aristotle. A Basenji, the unique breed originating in central Africa, washes itself like a cat, has no bark, and is depicted on the tombs of Pharaohs who believed the dog's expression hinted at inner wisdom and antiquity. As he glanced at the time on his clock radio, he suddenly realized how long he'd been asleep. *My God, it's 9:30. I'd better get going.*

His wife had left a heart-shaped note next to his pillow. It read, *you looked so content, my sleeping darling, I didn't have the heart to awaken you. There's fresh coffee in the thermos and bagels on the counter. I'll be home around seven. Love B__*

Raising the card to his nose, McClure inhaled the scent of her perfume and smiled. *Too bad she's not here.*

Invigorated by a hot shower, as he shaved, he gazed at the image reflected in a full-length bathroom mirror. Seeing dark circles under his eyes, he admonished himself. *You need more potassium, Harry.*

McClure descended one flight down a wrought iron staircase connecting his penthouse apartment to his office and approached the desk Velma Baker, his executive assistant and office manager.

An attractive 40-year-old African American woman, widowed, and the mother of a teenage boy, as McClure's dedicated gatekeeper she often used her seductive voice and charm to garner information or soothe the bruised ego of a chief executive or government official.

Her black hair pulled stylishly back from her face, Velma lifted her gaze and flashed an engaging smile.

"Good morning. How are you?" she asked.

McClure nodded. "I'm alright."

"How'd it go?

"Went well."

"Been in touch with Saunders McGee?"

"Yes, on the flight back, I called him on the satellite phone. He seemed quite pleased that we got all his people out unharmed."

The corner of her lips curling into a sly smile, Velma said, "I'm sure he's more than pleased."

McClure shot her a surprised look. "You are?"

"Well—about an hour ago a messenger delivered a wooden box tied with an elegant Bethlehem Oil red and blue ribbon. It's in your office."

Shaking his head, McClure grinned. "What would I do without you?"

Velma beamed.

"Is anything else pressing?"

"Mr. Davidov called from Jerusalem. He said he'd call back at ten-thirty."

McClure glanced at his watch and nodded. "Buzz me when he calls."

Velma had placed the wooden box on a table close to McClure's desk. Reaching for the monogrammed envelope, he opened it and read the handwritten note. *Harry, I knew I could count on you. Well done, and many thanks from all of us at Bethlehem Oil. Signed Saunders McGee.* As token of his appreciation, Bethlehem Chairman McGee had sent McClure a case of 18-year-old Glenmorangie Scotch.

McClure had earned a sizeable fee for his services, but nevertheless he appreciated McGee's gesture. As he was about to inspect one of the bottles, he glanced up at a TV monitor mounted to a wall tuned to CNN. The network had interrupted their regular news program with a special live bulletin from Jerusalem. He picked up the remote control and turned up the volume.

A uniformed Israeli police spokesman was addressing a group of international journalists. "At eight-thirty this morning, the bloodied body of Finance Minister Uzi Kopelman was discovered in an alleyway of the Jewish Quarter. An initial medical examination has determined massive internal hemorrhaging, resulting from a knife wound he sustained to his chest several hours earlier, as the probable cause of death. Pending a full investigation, we have no further details to report."

McClure muted the TV, and retrieved a handful of macadamia nuts from a jar on his desk. Popping several into his mouth, he wondered whether Davidov's call was related to the murder of Israel's Finance Minister. As he reflected, his thoughts flashed back to an earlier time in his life.

In 1973, while serving as a naval intelligence attaché assigned to the American Embassy in Tel Aviv, McClure first met his Israeli counterpart, Colonel Ariel Davidov. Although they had served together on a joint American/Israeli intelligence committee, it was their daily interaction during the Entebbe Incident that cemented their personal and professional relationship.

On June 27, 1976, soon after takeoff from Athens, terrorists hijacked an Air France Airbus A300 carrying 248 passengers, many of whom were Israeli nationals, and forced the pilot to land at Entebbe Airport in Uganda.

While a Special Forces unit of the Israeli Defense Forces (IDF) prepared to launch a covert mission aimed at rescuing the passengers, McClure arranged for a Mossad intelligence team to view American satellite reconnaissance photographs of the Entebbe Airport and the surrounding terrain.

His musing suddenly interrupted by Velma buzzing on the intercom, McClure pressed his index finger against the lighted button on his desk phone.

"Yes?"

"Mr. Davidov is on line one."

"I'll take it."

CHAPTER **3**

M
cClure raised the phone receiver to his ear.
"Hello, Ari. How are you?"
The former IDF Major General responsible for
overseeing Israel's intelligence agencies, his voice unusually
somber, replied, "I don't know if you've heard, but the body
of our Finance Minister, Uzi Kopelman, was found early this
morning in an alleyway of the Jewish quarter."

"Yes, I know. A few minutes before you called, I caught
part of a CNN Jerusalem news bulletin. Has anyone claimed
responsibility?"

"No one has come forward, so the media is labeling his
brutal murder a random act of terrorism." Davidov inhaled.
"But I'm not so sure."

"What do you mean?"

"Uzi was a big, powerful man. I'm certain he would have
put up a fight, but there were no marks on his body that

would indicate a struggle occurred. When he called yesterday, he said he needed to see me as soon as possible concerning a matter of national security. We had arranged to meet at my office at eight this morning, but he never arrived."

Davidov cleared his throat and added, "The initial police report states he probably died as a result of a knife wound to the chest. What perplexes me, however, is that a sample of his blood showed an unusually high level of d-tubocurarine."

McClure shot back, "That's the active ingredient in curare."

For a moment, Davidov chuckled. "I should've known you'd be familiar with curare."

"Since you found high levels of d-tubocurarine in Kopelman's blood sample, I suspect muscle and respiratory paralysis had already set in before he was stabbed. It may also account for why there's no evidence of a struggle."

"Your insight reinforces my theory. Whoever killed Uzi Kopelman intended his murder to appear as a random terrorist attack. The question is why—and is it related to his request to meet with me this morning?"

"I'm intrigued. Do you have any clues?"

"Only one and I'm not sure it's related."

"What've you got?"

"In Kopelman's shirt pocket, we found a blood-stained card. High-powered imaging revealed the smudged name, M. Rubin, USA, and three concentric purple lines. We haven't completed a thorough search of our database, but we did find an airport entry for a Mayer Rubin who visited Israel on an American passport two months ago. Could be a coincidence; maybe not."

"I'd say it's worth investigating."

"I agree, Harry. So, while we search our database and our cryptology department attempts to decipher the meaning of the three concentric purple lines, I'd like you to conduct a search for an M. Rubin who may be living in the United States. I'm especially interested in someone who may have visited Israel in the last twelve months."

"Anything else I should know?"

"Yes, there is . . . Uzi Kopelman was more than Israel's Finance Minister—he was a close friend who served as my chief of staff during the Yom Kippur War. I want you to help me track down the people responsible for his death."

Sensing the anguish in Davidov's voice, McClure replied confidently, "I understand, Ari. If the M. Rubin you seek is in the U.S., we'll find him. I'll be in touch."

"Thanks, Harry. Shalom."

Later in the afternoon, McClure briefed his Director of Field Operations, Robert L. Jones, on the call he received earlier in the day from Ariel Davidov.

"Without any witnesses and no one claiming responsibility for the Finance Minister's death, the words M. Rubin, USA and three concentric purple lines on the back of a bloodstained card found at the crime scene are our only clues."

Jones, the former head of the FBI's organized crime task force who had joined McClure's firm six months earlier, sensed McClure had a new assignment for him.

"As a first step, Bob, I want you to identify and profile all the M. Rubins living in the United States."

Jones nodded. "That shouldn't be too difficult, but what are we really looking for, Harry?"

McClure leaned forward and folded his hands on his desk. "I'm not sure, but whoever is responsible for the murder of the Finance Minister has gone to great lengths to hide their own identity. Is M. Rubin an American link to them? Let's find out."

# CHAPTER 4

A week later, at 6:30 p.m., McClure leaned back in his Herman Miller Aeron desk chair reviewing a confidential security proposal. The document, prepared by his director of international operations for a multinational oil company, recommended procedures for safeguarding key management from the threat of terrorist attacks and kidnappings in the Middle East.

As he finished penciling several comments in the margin of the memo, Velma approached his desk and handed him a red dossier.

"I'm leaving for the evening, but I thought you'd want to see this right away."

McClure eyed the cover and nodded. "I've been waiting for Jones's report. Thanks. See you in the morning."

Before opening the dossier, he read the note Jones had attached to the cover. *Margo Lang researched much of the material in the Mayer Rubin file. I'll be at a conference in Washington for the next two days, so, if you have any questions, don't hesitate to call her.*

To enhance his department's Middle East expertise, Jones had recently recruited Margo Lang. A skillful researcher, the former CIA profiles analyst held a Ph.D. in Middle-Eastern languages and was fluent in Hebrew, Arabic, Farsi, French and German.

McClure opened the dossier and scanned the contents page. He then read the two-page summary, skimmed pages three to nine, and turned to page 10. Having identified one or more M. Rubins residing in every state except Utah, Vermont, and Wyoming, Jones's team had narrowed the High Probability Profiles down to three men: Alan M. Rubin, Mayer Rubin, and Mordecai Rubin.

Each profile contained the individual's name, occupation, address, age, business background, and the number of times he visited Israel in the last year. While each of the three men potentially fit Davidov's criteria, it was the company name NovoMed, mentioned in Mayer Rubin's profile, which caught McClure's eye. The dossier noted, "Instrumental in organizing funding for an early stage medical products company, NovoMed, Board Member 1986–1989."

What a coincidence. *That's Max Eisen's company,* McClure had run into Max Eisen 10 days earlier as he walked along New York's Madison Avenue. Although they had been out of touch for many years, they warmly greeted each other.

After chatting for 10 minutes, they had exchanged business cards and set a date to meet for dinner.

Before closing the dossier, he thumbed the pages to the section dealing with Mayer Rubin's family: Both parents, Holocaust survivors. Mother, (Eva), née, Oppenheimer, born Berlin, Germany, May 13, 1920. Family: prominent German Jewish banking family . . . Grandfather, well known for organizing critical financing for Kaiser Wilhelm's war machine before and during World War 1 . . . First cousin of famed Jewish banker, S. Bleichroeder . . . As Private Finance Minister to Otto von Bismarck, Bleichroeder helped Bismarck consolidate a collection of independent states into a single entity that evolved into modern Germany.

Tapping his fingers on his rosewood desk, McClure reflected. *Quite a distinguished banking family. I'll bet, as loyal Germans, the Oppenheimers never imagined their country would ultimately betray them.*

He jotted a note to Jones, then tossed it into his outbox and retrieved a yellow Post-it reminder note Velma had stuck to his calendar. As he read the note, "Dinner with Max Eisen, 7:30, LaRosa," he thought of Ariel Davidov's phone call seven days earlier. *I wonder what Max can tell me about Mayer Rubin?*

# CHAPTER 5

As he neared the silver limousine parked in front of his brownstone offices, McClure was greeted by the familiar voice of his Jamaican chauffeur, Owen Mills. They chatted briefly, then McClure slipped into the backseat.

Viewing his boss through the rear view mirror, his chauffeur asked, "Where we heading tonight?"

"LaRosa on Third Avenue."

The chauffeur nodded. "Not much traffic tonight. Won't take long."

While McClure's eyes followed the seductive display of colored neon lights illuminating New York City as day turned to night, he thought of the years he served as a security consultant for the international conglomerate Equinox Communications. Working and traveling with Max Eisen, then Equinox's Vice President of International Development, they had developed a close business and personal relationship. But soon after Max left Equinox, they drifted apart.

Upon entering the restaurant, McClure noted a long line of patrons awaiting tables. Undeterred, he casually pushed his way to the front of the line. Immediately recognizing him, the maitre d' greeted him with a warm smile. "Nice seeing you again, Mr. McClure. You have a gentleman waiting for you at your table."

McClure handed his tan Burberry trench coat to an attendant, then followed a few steps behind the maitre d' as he deftly parted a path through the crowded dining room. "Here we are. Your waiter will be with you shortly."

As he eyed the man sitting at his favorite table, McClure unobtrusively pressed a crisp folded ten-dollar bill into the maitre d's palm.

"Good evening, Max."

A trim 5'10", Max Eisen had fair complexion and defined angular features, and wore tortoise-rimmed glasses that partially concealed intense blue eyes. Springing from his chair, he grasped McClure's outstretched hand. "How are you?" he asked, smiling.

"I'm fine. Waiting long?"

"No. I got here five minutes ago."

As they conversed, a tall dark-haired waiter appeared at their table. "Gentlemen, can I get you a drink?"

McClure turned to Max. "What's your pleasure?"

"I'll have Glenmorangie with a splash of water."

McClure smiled approvingly.

"And for you, Mr. McClure?" the waiter asked.

"I'll have the same."

A short time later, the waiter placed their drinks on the table. After he jotted down their dinner order, he turned to McClure. "Have you selected a wine?"

"Bring us a bottle of 1989 Prunotto Barolo Cannubi."

Fifteen minutes later, as they reminisced over the many adventures they had shared at Equinox Communications, the waiter returned with a wine bottle.

McClure scanned the label, then nodded. The waiter removed the cork, placed it in front of McClure's plate, and poured a small amount of wine into his glass. Lifting the glass, his head tilted slightly back, McClure sampled the wine. Satisfied, he signaled the waiter to pour.

Raising his wine glass, McClure fixed his eyes on Max. "Here's to your company's success!"

"I'll drink to that," Max said, raising his glass to his mouth. As he set his wine glass on the white linen tablecloth, he smiled. "Superb!"

They continued chatting for several minutes, then Max leaned back in his chair. "Still consulting for EC?"

"No, I'm not. That part of my life ended when Vista International acquired Equinox. Anyway, my life dramatically changed after my accident."

A surprised look on his face, Max asked, "What happened?"

"I was involved in a nasty head-on collision on the Henry Hudson Parkway. One of those accidents you read about, but never imagine could happen to you. An oncoming car jumped the median and slammed into me. The police later said the driver was killed instantly."

"My God. You were lucky."

"I was more than lucky. Miraculously, firemen, using the Jaws of Life, pried me from the wreckage. Thanks to a remarkable nurse who cared for me at Columbia-Presbyterian Hospital, I made a speedy recovery." McClure smiled, then added, "A year later, we were married."

"Congratulations," Max said, raising his wine glass.

"Thanks. You'll get to meet Bernadette before too long."

Moments after the waiter placed their dinner plates on the table, McClure motioned to Max. "Let's eat."

Although anxious to explore the extent of Mayer Rubin's involvement in NovoMed, McClure waited until their waiter cleared the dinner plates before asking, "How's your company doing?"

Max gave a pained smile. "I'll be candid. We've developed an innovative medical system that's been cleared by the FDA for marketing."

"Sounds exciting."

"It is. But I have a problem."

"Oh, what kind of problem?"

Max sighed. "My intent to complete a new round of financing is being undermined by someone who's manipulating our publicly traded stock. Without new capital, I'm dead in the water."

"Any thought who it might be?"

"I can't be sure," Max said, frowning, "but I've got a hunch one of my former directors is involved."

McClure cocked an eyebrow. "A former director?"

"Yeah, his name is Mayer Rubin."

Although surprised by Max's statement, McClure avoided any expression or comment that might reveal his own interest in Mayer Rubin. Instead, he calmly asked, "How did Mayer Rubin get involved with NovoMed?"

Max groaned. "It's a long story."

"Then start from the beginning," McClure said, with an encouraging wave of his hand.

"When I left Equinox, I started a consulting business with an old Wall Street friend. At a board meeting of a company we had helped raise capital, I overheard the president of the company mention a doctor who had patented a unique technology for predicting a potential heart attack, twenty-four to thirty-six hours before it occurs."

"Wait a minute," McClure interjected, "you mean to tell me that someone has invented a way to predict a heart attack before it occurs?"

"That's right. There's new computer-based technology available for assessing the probability of an imminent heart attack. Like you, when I first heard of the technology, I was intrigued, but skeptical, so I contacted the inventor, Dr.

Michael Darmin. After a half hour telephone discussion, we agreed to meet at my office the following week."

McClure nodded. "And—"

"We discussed his patent, which he said included a proprietary method of collecting and transmitting an individual's critical vital signs to a central station for interpretation by a computer algorithm, then moved on to how we might help him raise the capital he needed. However, when I told him we only engage clients on an exclusive contractual basis, he responded by saying he expected to close on venture capital funding within several weeks. If that's the case, I said, good luck!"

"How did he react?"

"Dr. Darmin sprang from his chair and stormed out without even saying goodbye. I didn't expect I'd hear from him again, but a month later he called and asked if I'd consider raising the funds he needed. Obviously, his funding plans didn't work out."

"Dr. Darmin sounds like quite a character."

"Yes, but recognizing the potential of the technology, I decided to listen to what he had to say. This time after asking only one additional question, he agreed to my conditions."

"Now I'm curious. What was his question?"

"He wanted to know if I thought the new company had the potential to go public."

McClure shook his head and laughed. "Greedy bastard."

"I agree, but, excited by the project's potential, I prepared and circulated a private placement memorandum to several of our regular funding sources. Surprisingly, they all turned it down. Discouraged by months of presentations without any commitments, I was ready to call it quits. Then something unexpected occurred.

"I was at a meeting with Clark Myers, a partner at Simms and Company. They're a small boutique investment firm which has made a name for itself funding and underwriting promising new technology companies."

"Yes, I know the firm," McClure interjected.

Max continued. "When the meeting ended Clark asked me to stay. He told me he knew an individual who had expressed interest in financing the Vital Signs Monitoring System, and asked if I would like to meet him. Sure, I responded. 'This individual,' he added, 'is, let's say, not your typical venture capitalist.'

"A little miffed, I asked, what do you mean not typical? Lowering his voice, Clark replied, 'he's a Hasid.' Pretending not to notice the uncomfortable expression on his face, I asked how he knew Mayer Rubin. He said he'd met him a year earlier and that Mayer Rubin had invested in several deals managed by his firm."

"So that's how you met Mayer Rubin."

That's right. I met Mayer Rubin for the first time in the conference room of the WASP investment firm of Simms and Company. But there's more—"

Before Max could elaborate, the waiter approached their table. "I'm sorry to interrupt you, Mr. McClure, but the kitchen is closing. Is there anything else I can get you?"

"No, we're fine. You can bring the check."

As he looked around the restaurant, McClure realized that he and Max were the only customers. Turning to Max, he said, "I know we had a lot to catch up on tonight, but I'd like to hear more about Mayer Rubin and NovoMed. Perhaps I can be of some help to you."

Max smiled. "I was hoping you'd say that, Harry."

McClure folded his napkin and set it down on the table. *I need to know more about Mayer Rubin.* Eying Max, he said, "I've got an idea. If you're free this weekend, how about joining me at my country house in the Catskills? We can get in some fishing and discuss your company and Mayer Rubin at length."

"Sounds good."

"Excellent. Velma will fax you driving directions in the morning."

McClure scanned the bill, added a generous tip, and signed his name diagonally across the face of the check. As they exited onto Third Avenue, he extended his arm and shook Max's hand. "It's been a great evening. See you on Saturday."

# CHAPTER 6

**M**ax Eisen rose early on Saturday morning. He hadn't slept well. An entrepreneur, he had for nearly five years devoted his energies to building NovoMed into an innovative medical technology company, but the disturbing pattern of rumors and unexplained swings in his company's publicly traded stock now threatened its survival. The stakes were high for Max. Though on paper he had a personal worth of more than 10 million dollars, he knew if his company failed, his stock would be worthless.

Careful not to awaken his wife, he quietly packed an overnight bag. Before departing, he gazed at her and gently kissed her cheek. She sighed. Smiling, he recalled the mornings, as he prepared to leave for work, she would awaken and they would embrace. Today was different. He had much on his mind and knew she would sense his anguish. Carefully opening the bedroom door, he quietly exited.

Stimulated by the cool early spring morning air, he steered his Saab convertible through Ridgewood, NJ and onto Route 17 North. As he merged onto the New York State Thruway, he inserted a Johnny Cash CD into the car's enhanced sound system and accelerated the turbo-powered engine. Leaving the thruway at Exit 16 Harriman, he then headed west on Route 17 toward Monticello for 17.8 miles until reaching a secondary road called Newton Corners. There he turned right and located a driveway marked by a splayed red cross. *That's odd*, he thought. *McClure was never religious, or was he?*

Max continued for several miles on a dirt road through a dense pine forest until he reached an open field. On the far side of the field, he could see several Adirondack-style buildings and a large red barn. Stopping his car in front of the main house, he spotted McClure dressed in blue jeans and a red shirt, waving. As he stepped out of his car, McClure greeted him with a broad smile.

"Directions okay?"

"Yes, they were fine, but what's the deal with the splayed red cross on the sign post marker?"

"Oh, that—" McClure laughed. "It's a vestige of another time. I'll tell you about it later. Let's go inside."

McClure led Max into a foyer filled with turn-of-the-century memorabilia that opened into a great room dominated by a large stone fireplace topped with a hearth of three-inch smoke-blue quarried slate. A row of tall mullioned windows facing north on the far side of the room accentuated the massive hand-hewn beams and trusses supporting the roof.

Max scanned the large room, then, holding back a smile, said, "Quite a country house."

"Thanks," McClure replied modestly. "It was built in 1910 by a prominent sugar merchant, Cyrus Brown. He loved the Adirondacks, but wanted a place closer to the city where he could entertain his wealthy friends. Interestingly, I've discovered the house contains many unusual devices and secret passageways."

Leading the way up an ornate mahogany staircase to the second floor, McClure guided Max down a hallway lit by antique wall lamps and opened the door to a spacious room facing an open meadow. Diffused light pouring in through large chestnut-trimmed windows, combined with Adirondack style furniture, gave the room a warm, comfortable ambiance.

"Join me downstairs when you're ready."

Max nodded. "I won't be long."

The guest room brought back memories of the college summers Max had worked as an Adirondack guide. He had visited many of the "Great Camps" built in the early 1900's by wealthy entrepreneurs, so when he opened the bathroom door, he chuckled. *I've seen these before.*

In the corner of the white-tiled room stood a vintage marble toilet with a pull-cord attached to a brown wooden box mounted to the wall near the ceiling. Pulling the cord released a volume of water collected in the box, which flushed the toilet. Interested in turn–of-the century history and gadgets, Max knew the device was named for Sir Thomas Crapper, a well-known Victorian plumber, who though not the inventor, successfully marketed the Silent Valveless Water Waste Preventer, which came to be known as a "Crapper."

Max closed the door behind him and strode down the mahogany staircase. At the main floor landing, McClure waited.

"My housekeeper, Elsa, prepared lunch for us to take along. Why don't you grab the thermos, and I'll take the cooler. The fishing gear is in the jeep parked outside."

McClure started the jeep's engine. "Won't take us long to get to the lake. You'll see. It's a gem."

CHAPTER 7

**M**cClure drove his vintage jeep along a private gravel road for nearly a mile, then turned onto a narrow dirt road that meandered through a hardwood forest. As the road spilled into a clearing, Max got his first glimpse of the pristine eight-mile lake that had formed in prehistoric times.

"Wow! You weren't kidding, Harry."

Gesturing with his hand, McClure drew Max's attention to the small steamboat moored to the dock.

Max removed his sunglasses and inspected the boat. "Reminds me of a boat I've seen at the Adirondack Museum."

"Yes, I know the one you're referring to. It's a similar boat once owned by William W. Durant. At the turn-of-the-century, he was the primary developer of large tracts of land in the Adirondack wilderness. Boats of this kind were popular toys of wealthy entrepreneurs who commissioned Durant to construct grand lodges on secluded Adirondack lakes. Only a few boats are still around." McClure pointed to a blue-grey painted Victorian era boathouse facing the lake. "See that building?"

Max turned and gazed at the boathouse.

"Shortly after I acquired the property, I found the steamboat inside the boathouse. The hull and body were in relatively good shape, but the engine needed an overhaul. No one around here knew anything about fixing it, but, luckily, I found an old timer living on Saranac Lake who knew everything there was to know about these antique boats. He wouldn't come here, so I had it hauled up to him."

Shaking his head, Max laughed. "You're amazing!"

McClure smiled and continued. "When I went to pick the boat up the following spring, he insisted I take it for a spin on the lake. The moment the engine started, I knew I had a great boat."

McClure started the engine and for several minutes patiently monitored the needle of a brass pressure gauge mounted to a bracket in front of the steering wheel. When sufficient steam had built up in the small boiler, he called out to Max, "Untie the lines and climb aboard."

While Max untied the mooring lines, McClure pulled on a wooden-handled cord that released a burst of steam, activating the boat's deep resonating horn. Slowly pushing the throttle forward, he piloted the steamboat onto the lake. As they approached a cove, he killed the engine and dropped anchor. "Let's get the fishing gear out and have some lunch."

By late afternoon, the sun peeking through a low cloud in the western sky, Max thought his catch was more than enough for the day. Suddenly, a strong tug on his line changed his mind. The powerful fish, a large bass, fought valiantly, but Max skillfully reeled it in.

Proud of Max's achievement, McClure grabbed two cold beers from the cooler and handed one to Max. "You may have caught the biggest bass in the lake. Cheers."

A short time later, both men in high spirits, McClure gazed at Max. "I meant to tell you. After our dinner, I got to thinking about NovoMed, so I pulled your most recent 10K filing."

"Oh?"

McClure nodded. "In reading it, I noticed something unusual."

Max's eyes narrowed. "What was it?"

"The former director you mentioned the other night, Mayer Rubin, who's also one of your largest shareholders, transferred a sizeable chunk of his company stock to a Brooklyn yeshiva last year."

"Yes, and he's done that more than once."

"Did you ask him why he transferred so much of his stock to a yeshiva?"

"Sure, I asked him. He told me it was a donation to further 'God's work.' Max's jaw tightened, then he added in a derisive tone, "A short time after the yeshiva was issued new unrestricted stock certificates, they sold their shares."

"And what was your counsel's opinion?"

"He said that, since Mayer no longer owned the shares, it was perfectly legal for the yeshiva to sell."

McClure gave a skeptical smile. "From what I've heard, there's a lot more I'd like to know about Mayer Rubin and his relationship with NovoMed. It's 4:30, so let's head back and continue our discussion over dinner."

Max nodded. "I'll get our gear together."

McClure started the boat's engine. In a few minutes, a full head of steam built up, he pushed the throttle forward, and the graceful boat got underway. As they approached the shore, he let up on the throttle, reversed the engine, and eased to a complete stop a few inches parallel to the dock. Jumping onto the dock, Max secured the bow and stern mooring lines. Seeing the somber expression on Max's face as he handed him their gear, McClure flashed a playful smile. "Well done, Max. You're a worthy mate."

Max's expression lightened, then he grinned. "Thanks, captain."

## CHAPTER 8

As he parked the jeep behind the house, McClure said to Max, "You take the fish cooler and I'll grab the gear." When they entered the kitchen, Elsa, who was preparing bread dough on a marble-topped kitchen table, rinsed her hands and drifted over to them.

How'd the fishing go?" she asked.

McClure looked at Max. "Show her what you've caught."

Max opened the cooler and pulled out the large bass.

"My, that's a big fish," Elsa said, smiling. "I'll take care of it for you. It'll be ready before you leave tomorrow."

Max thanked her, then he and McClure walked from the kitchen to the foyer. Max stopped in front of a large John Singer Sargent print portraying blindfolded English soldiers who had been exposed to mustard gas during World War I. He studied the impressive print, then turned to McClure.

"I've seen the original oil painting at the Imperial War Museum in London. I like Sargent's work."

McClure nodded. "I too, am a fan of his. This print is the same size as the original painting and one of only twenty-five Sargent commissioned and gave to special friends. My Scottish grandfather, a distinguished surgeon who served as a major in the English Army during World War I, was one of those recipients. It's been in our family ever since."

They continued discussing World War I for more than 10 minutes, then McClure said, "I've got a few things I need to take care of. Let's meet at seven for a drink before dinner."

When he opened the door to his room, Max sensed the fragrance of fresh lavender. *Nice touch, Elsa.* Slipping off his shoes, he set his wristwatch alarm and lowered onto a goose-down comforter draped over the bed. In less than a minute, he drifted into sleep.

At 6:15 p.m., awakened by the beeping sound of his wristwatch alarm, Max opened the bathroom door and pressed an antique light switch mounted to the bathroom wall. Instantly the brass lamp over the bathroom sink illuminated the white-tiled room with incandescent light. He opened the door to a glass-enclosed shower, turned the water on and plunged in after his outreached hand sensed a steady stream of hot water. The hot water invigorated him, but he didn't want to linger.

Reaching for the large white towel hanging on an antique brass hook, he dried himself and gazed at his image in the beveled mirror. As he applied lather to his face and began to shave, he thought of Mayer Rubin.

"Fuck," he cried out, feeling a sharp sting on his face and seeing droplets of blood appear in the white porcelain sink. Preoccupied with his business problems, he had applied undue pressure to the razor. He grabbed a styptic pencil from his travel bag, moistened its tip under the running water and applied it to the nick on his face. The bleeding stopped. For a moment he admonished himself. *Why wasn't I smarter in my dealings with Mayer Rubin?* Regaining his composure, he finished shaving, dried his face, and splashed on a few drops of aftershave lotion. Once dressed, he headed downstairs to join McClure.

When they finished dinner, Elsa cleared the table. A few minutes later, she returned with a cheesecake topped with wild blueberries and a carafe of coffee. After serving the cake and pouring coffee, she looked at McClure. "Can I get you anything else?"

"Thanks, Elsa," McClure replied with an appreciative smile. "We'll be fine."

McClure added a lump of sugar to his cup. As he stirred the coffee, he gazed at Max. "Tell me about your initial contact with Mayer Rubin."

Max nodded, took a sip of coffee, then set the cup on a white saucer. "I can clearly remember our first meeting. When I opened the conference room door, my eyes were drawn to a short, stocky, bearded man wearing a large black hat. He was making notes in a small notebook. When he saw me, he stopped writing and slowly moved in my direction. As I shook his weak outstretched hand, I noticed, under thick wire-rimmed glasses, two small dark brown eyes focused on me."

Max took another sip of coffee and continued. "He said he understood I was seeking funds for a startup medical company. After about twenty-five minutes of discussion, I asked if he'd ever invested in medical startups. He nodded and said he had. He then handed me a business card and requested I overnight a business plan to him. Later in the day, when I checked the address on his card, I realized Mayer Rubin was a member of the Bobov Hasidic Community in Boro Park, Brooklyn."

While McClure listened to Max's narrative of Mayer Rubin, he again thought of his assignment for Ari Davidov. *Could Mayer's financial dealings be the key?* "Let's take a break and continue in the library."

# CHAPTER 9

M cClure's library boasted a chestnut tongue-and-groove ceiling and tall windows. A reflection of his personal and professional interests, it contained an eclectic collection of historical and fictional works, many rare and first editions.

Motioning toward the Adirondack-style furniture arranged around a large stone fireplace, McClure said, "Take your pick."

As Max lowered into a high backed upholstered chair, he observed McClure press his thumb against a tarnished plaque depicting a medieval knight on horseback clutching a shield emblazoned with a splayed red cross. To his astonishment, a moment later, a concealed wooden panel slowly swung away from the wall, revealing an interior room.

"Amazing!" Max exclaimed, bolting from his chair. "But how did you know that pressing your thumb against the plaque would open the panel?"

"Actually, it was quite by chance. A few weeks after I closed on the house, I discovered an old wooden chest stored in the back of the attic, probably overlooked by the moving crew when they cleaned it out. When I opened the chest, I found a black leather-bound book embossed with an eye inside a triangle. On the first page, it said the book had been presented to Cyrus Brown on the day of his initiation as a 33rd degree Freemason on July 7, 1917."

"That's fascinating."

"It is, but there's more. On the last page, I found a note describing how to access a secret room in the library. I couldn't wait to find out, so I headed to the library and located the plaque. Following the instructions, I pressed my thumb on the splayed red cross within the shield of the Templar Knight. A moment later, hearing a grinding sound, I watched as one of the wall panels swung away from the wall, revealing a secret room.

"I was surprised to find the room contained several large steamer trunks filled with books, records, and memorabilia related to the Knights Templar and the Freemasons. Come, take a look."

Peering into the large, dimly lit, windowless room, Max eyed a faded image painted on the wall in front of him, a compass positioned over a mason's square with the letter "G" inscribed in the center of the two instruments. "What do the symbols mean?"

"What you're looking at are ancient Freemason symbols, the builders square and the compass. The "G" stands for "geometry" as well as "God." This room may have been used for secret Masonic meetings."

Max stared at the Masonic images for a long moment, then turned to McClure. "Weren't many of the founding fathers Freemasons?"

"They were. In fact, a number of the delegates who signed the Declaration of Independence, including Benjamin Franklin and John Hancock, were Freemasons. When George Washington took office as the first President of the United States, he was sworn in on a Masonic Bible. Freemasons, as I've learned since discovering this room, have woven many of their secret symbols and geometric patterns into the architecture of Washington, D.C."

"Have you looked at the other books you found in the steamer trunks?"

"Only a few. Many are old and written in an ornate style. One book contains a detailed description of Masonic rituals and handshakes. When I get some time, I plan to examine them more closely. I have a hunch there are a lot of Masonic secrets buried in those trunks."

Once again, McClure pressed his thumb against the splayed Red Cross on the shield of the Templar Knight. A moment later, the panel swung back into the wall.

An amused smile on his face, Max said, "Now I understand the significance of the marker at the entrance of your driveway."

McClure winked, then reached for a mahogany humidor and opened the lid. "Cigar?"

"Sure." Max selected a full-sized Cuban Cohiba, snipped off the tip, lit it with a cedar match and inhaled. "Nice."

McClure lit a cigar and focused his gaze on Max. "Now let's continue from where we left off on Mayer Rubin."

Max nodded. "A few days later Mayer called. He said he had reviewed the business plan and was interested in getting together again when he returned from Israel in two weeks. Jotting down the date in my calendar, I noted he had scheduled our next meeting two days after the end of Passover. Sure enough, when he returned from Israel, he called and asked if I could arrange a meeting with Dr. Darmin. That's how it all began."

McClure puffed on his cigar, then set it down in an ashtray. "I've got to say, from what I've heard so far, it doesn't sound all that bad to me."

"You're right, but that was five years ago. NovoMed was still a private company. After we went public two-and-a-half years ago—that's when I noticed a change."

"What do you mean?"

"Well, up to that point we had no problem keeping internal discussions of our marketing plans, financial projections, or contracts in negotiation confidential. Then, suddenly, information not available to the public and often inflated and taken out of context began appearing in Internet chat rooms and financial newsletters."

"And you think Mayer Rubin is somehow connected to the leaks?"

"I can't be sure, but many times after an inflated story circulated, our stock would mysteriously rise to a new high, sometimes by as much as twenty-five percent. A day or so later, the stock Mayer had earlier transferred, or what he liked to say, 'donated' to a yeshiva was sold."

"What effect did the sale of the yeshiva stock have on the value of NovoMed's stock?"

Max sneered. "Within a few days, the stock would retreat to the level it sold for prior to the run up. For days after, irate investors would call seeking an explanation for why the stock had tumbled."

Hearing the ornate grandfather clock in the hallway chime once, McClure rose and emptied his ashtray into the fireplace. *Mayer Rubin is a bigger player than I thought.* He then turned and faced Max. "Mayer Rubin may be responsible for manipulating your company's stock, but until we have concrete proof, we can't pin anything on him. Let's get some rest and continue in the morning."

## CHAPTER 10

Max awoke the next morning to the aroma of freshly brewed coffee drifting up to his room from the kitchen below. Anxious to continue discussions with McClure, he quickly showered and dressed. Downstairs, in a sunny corner of the kitchen, sitting at a chestnut table, was McClure, coffee cup in hand, immersed in the *Sunday New York Times.*

"Good morning, Harry."

Looking up, McClure smiled. "Good morning. Sleep well?"

Max nodded. "I did."

"Coffee?"

"Just what I need."

From a bright red thermal carafe, McClure filled a large blue and white china cup and pointed to the cream and sugar.

"Max, I've been thinking about our discussion last night. Your comment that confidential financial and marketing plans are mysteriously finding their way to Internet chat rooms and financial newsletters troubles me. I wonder. Is someone within your company passing on information?" McClure paused. "Or is there another explanation?"

A puzzled look on his face, Max said, "What are you thinking?"

McClure formed a steeple with his fingertips and gazed at Max intently. "I hope I'm wrong, but I have a hunch your offices are bugged."

Surprised, Max recoiled. "Our offices bugged?"

"I can't be certain, but I've seen similar scenarios before. I suggest we conduct an electronic sweep of your offices as soon as possible."

Max sighed. "Sure."

"How's Tuesday morning?"

"That's fine."

"My director of field operations, Robert Jones, will send a team to your office. He joined my company six months ago after retiring from the FBI. His department installed many of the bugging devices used to collect evidence on members of the mob. If there are any bugs in your office, his men will find them. We should then plan on meeting later in the week. How's Thursday?"

Max checked his pocket planner. "Thursday isn't good. I've got a meeting with a hospital group in Tampa, but Friday is okay."

"That'll work. Let's meet at my office at two-thirty on Friday. In the meantime, I want you to FedEx me all of your 10Ks and 10Qs. I'll also need copies of all of your corporate minutes, press releases, and incorporation documents."

Max nodded and jotted down the list of records McClure requested. "You'll have them in a few days."

Two hours later, as Max prepared to leave, McClure presented him with a cooler filled with the cleaned and frozen fish they had caught the day before.

"How can I thank you?"

McClure smiled and threw up his hands. "Don't thank me. It's a gift from Elsa."

Max loaded the cooler and his travel bag into the Saab's rear compartment and closed the hatch door. Turning to McClure, his expression serious, he said, "It's been a great weekend, and I appreciate your offer to help me, but . . . do you think I'm being a bit too paranoid about Mayer Rubin?"

Gazing at Max, McClure thought, *I've never seen him so distraught.* Placing his hand on Max's shoulder, he replied, "I don't think so. From what you've told me, it's clear that someone is sabotaging your company. At this point, although we can't be certain Mayer Rubin is involved, we do know that a number of his past actions are, at the least, suspect. Until we can rule him out, let's continue investigating Mr. Rubin."

Max nodded and shook McClure's hand. "Thanks, Harry. I'll see you on Friday."

While McClure watched Max's car glide across the open meadow and disappear into the forest, he made a mental note. *Accelerate Jones's investigation of Mayer Rubin.*

# CHAPTER 11

Max Eisen's intercom buzzed. "Mr. Kearny is here to see you."

"I've been expecting him, Beth. Send him in."

Once again, Max's intercom buzzed. "Yes?"

"Mr. Kearny wants you to come out to the reception area."

Though puzzled, Max replied, "Tell him I'll be right out."

Max peered through the glass doors leading to the reception area and observed a tall, thin man in a dark blue suit gazing out of a row of tinted windows on the far side of the room. As Max approached him, the man abruptly turned in his direction and, his index finger pressed against his mouth, signaled Max to remain silent. Max nodded and silently followed the man to the outer hallway. There he introduced himself as Chet Kearny.

Apologizing, Kearny explained, "If there are any bugging devices in your offices, I don't want to tip off anyone who might be listening. To guard against anyone knowing of our work, I'll be back at six. In the meantime, I'll run a check in the building's telephone room."

At six sharp, hearing the door buzzer sound, Max unlocked the front door. Kearny was standing in the entranceway clutching an aluminum military-style attaché case.

Max watched as Kearny removed a small pad from his breast pocket and printed, *I'd like to check your office first.* He read the note, nodded, and motioned for Kearny to follow.

Inside Max's office, Kearny retrieved a wand-like device from a compartment within his attaché case. When he switched it on, two red diodes began to blink silently. Raising the wand, he passed it over and under a table lamp alongside Max's couch. The slow intermittent blinking of the red diodes remained constant as he lifted the wand and methodically moved it over, under, and around the couch.

Continuing in the same manner, Kearny passed the wand over a telephone on an end table, but the slow intermittent blinking of the red diodes remained constant. Unscrewing the caps on both ends of the telephone handset, he carefully examined the interior wiring. Satisfied, he reassembled the handset and moved over to Max's desk.

The red diodes on the wand blinked. As he moved closer to an antique lamp perched on the corner of Max's desk, the red diodes changed from blinking to a steady red. Kearny unscrewed the brass finial holding the shade in place and placed the shade upside down on the desk.

A pleased smile on his face, he pointed to a small object attached to the underside of the copper shade. Fishing into his pocket, he withdrew a Swiss army pocket knife, and peeled the object away from the shade. In his palm, he held a circular transistorized receiver the size of a dime.

Retrieving a small oval canister from within his attaché case, he removed the lid and foam insert. After placing the "bug" into the canister, he inserted the foam padding and closed the lid.

Stunned by Kearny's discovery, Max stared at the canister in silence.

Slowly moving the wand, Kearny continued to probe every corner of the room. Confident he had cleared all of the bugs in Max's office, he finally spoke. "Your office is clear for now."

Max pursed his lips. "Do you think there may be more bugs in other areas of the office?"

Kearny nodded. "Could be, but—" Before he could elaborate, the sound of the front door bell distracted him. "That's probably my assistant. We'll need a few hours to check the rest of your office, so there's no need for you to hang around. When we're done, we'll turn the lights off and lock the front door."

Although Max nodded his approval, silently he wondered, *what else are the people who bugged my office planning?*

# CHAPTER 12

When Max opened the door to his office the next morning, he immediately spotted a large tan folder marked IMPORTANT in bold red letters. In it, he found a memo from Steve Markham, NovoMed's vice president of biomedical engineering, indicating that his engineering team had successfully completed field testing of the telephonic vital signs monitoring system. Pleased by the positive news, Max reached for his phone, but as he lifted the receiver to dial Markham's extension, his assistant buzzed on the intercom.

"Mr. McClure is on line one."

"I'll take it."

Max pressed the phone to his ear. "Good morning. I guess you've heard that Jones's men discovered a bug in my office last night."

"I know, and after you left your office, they found a second bug in your conference room."

Max sighed. "Damn it. Do you have any idea who planted the bugs?"

"Not yet, but Jones is working on locating the monitoring station. We should have that information within a few days. In the meantime, I reviewed the initial private placement document you sent me. I'd like to discuss it when we meet on Friday. Do you have our new address?"

"I think so." Max pulled up his contact list on the computer screen. "110 East 57th Street?"

"That's it. By the way, do you have any photographs of Mayer Rubin and his cronies you can bring along?"

Max chuckled. "I'm sure I can dig some up."

"Fine, then I'll see you on Friday."

# CHAPTER 13

Max arrived at McClure's brownstone on East 57th Street at 1:30 p.m. Darting up five sandstone steps, he eyed a rectangular polished brass plate mounted to the right side of an imposing beveled glass and mahogany door. It read, McClure Associates, Ltd.

The brownstone served as both McClure's offices and city residence, the first two floors devoted to his business, while the top floor he shared with his wife Bernadette and their dog, Aristotle.

Acquired by McClure for a fraction of its real worth from a client in need of cash to settle an expensive divorce, the aged pinkish brown façade sharply contrasted with the modern interior. The offices, furnished with teak and rosewood Scandinavian furniture, were equipped with the latest computers, tech lighting, and a sophisticated communications system.

A moment after he pressed the illuminated button below the plaque, Max heard a woman's voice address him through a tiny speaker imbedded in the doorframe.

"Good afternoon, Mr. Eisen. I'll buzz you in."

As Max was about to reach for the ornate brass door handle, the door unexpectedly glided open on its own power. Passing through a narrow foyer, he entered a well-appointed reception area illuminated by four milk-glass-domed floor lamps. In the center of the room, a young blonde woman sat behind a rosewood desk. Making eye contact with Max, she rose from her desk and approached him.

"Hello," she said, smiling. "I'm Kristin. May I take your coat, Mr. Eisen?"

Max nodded. "Sure."

She motioned to the elevator and directed him to exit on the second floor. When the elevator door opened, Velma greeted him with a warm smile.

"Good afternoon, Mr. Eisen. We've been expecting you. Please come with me."

As he trailed close behind her along a hallway lit by recessed halogen lights, Max couldn't avoid noticing the graceful rhythmic movement of her well-proportioned body. Stopping in front of an office enclosed in blue-tinted glass, she said, "This is Mr. McClure's office. He's on the phone, but I'm sure he won't be long. Please have a seat in his lounge."

# CHAPTER 14

W hile Max waited for McClure, he browsed a wall displaying photographs of McClure in the company of prominent corporate executives, generals, and heads of state. To his surprise, at the end of the row he found a framed photograph of McClure and himself. Both men, in shorts and sunglasses, appeared dwarfed by a large swordfish they had caught on a fishing trip off the coast of the Dominican Republic. As he recalled the moment, a familiar voice called out to him.

"Max, come on in."

Adjacent to his office, McClure had installed a private conference room equipped with a state-of-the art communications system and real-time news feed. Over the oval rosewood conference table hung a circular glass-encased halogen fixture suspended from the ceiling by four thin wires.

Spread out on the conference table was the packet of NovoMed documents which Max had FedExed earlier in the week. McClure motioned to a carafe of coffee on a rosewood credenza. "Help yourself."

Max poured a cup of coffee and eased into a black leather chair. "Alright, where shall we begin?"

McClure eyed the NovoMed folder on the table in front of him. "Let's start with the individuals who were instrumental in organizing NovoMed."

Max pulled a file from his briefcase titled NovoMed Private Placement Memo and passed it to McClure.

"As you know, the key player is my former director, Mayer Rubin."

Raising an eyebrow, McClure challenged Max. "I know you mentioned Mayer Rubin is no longer a director of NovoMed, but why did he step down as a director?"

"We had a big blowout about a year ago."

"What happened?"

"I'd just returned from a meeting with a hospital group in Atlanta. I was scanning the front page of the *Wall Street Journal* when I noticed a headline: *Five Individuals Indicted by a Federal Grand Jury for Stock Manipulation and Fraud.*"

His eyes focused on Max, McClure leaned back in his chair and folded his hands together.

Max went on. "I was shocked to see Mayer Rubin's name mentioned in the article. Just as I finished reading, my assistant walked into my office. Noting the expression on my face, she asked what was wrong. I told her one of our directors was indicted by a federal grand jury."

"How'd she react?"

"Frowning, she asked who it was. When I told her it was Mayer Rubin, she drew her hand to her mouth and said she wasn't surprised. At that point, I asked her to get our corporate attorney, Mark Federman, on the line right away."

"Isn't Federman the attorney who represented Mayer Rubin when the company was organized?"

"He is. Sounding unperturbed, Federman said he was in a meeting and asked if he could call me back in about an hour. In the meantime, I called Mayer. His wife said he had gone out, but she would give him the message. About a half hour later, Mayer returned my call. I immediately asked if the allegations in the Wall Street Journal were true."

"What was his answer?"

"In typical form, he assured me there was no truth to the allegations and that he wasn't guilty of any of the charges. I wasn't convinced. By the afternoon, we had a flurry of calls from shareholders wanting to know what was going on with a board member."

"Did Federman call you back?"

"Yeah, a few minutes after I got off the phone with Mayer. He was very lawyer-like. We discussed the *Wall Street Journal* article and the potential repercussions for the company. He said in typical legalese jargon that on one hand Mayer hadn't been found guilty of any crime, but on the other hand his presence on the board might negatively affect the company's stock. In essence, he was leaving the decision up to me.

"At a stormy board meeting the following week, and only after Federman told him his resignation would be in the best interest of the company, did Mayer reluctantly agree to step down."

"Last weekend, you mentioned that Mayer Rubin, on several occasions, transferred large blocks of his personal company stock to several yeshivas in Brooklyn."

Max nodded.

"What are the rules governing the sale or transfer of founders stock to a third party?"

Max thought for a moment. "Founding shareholders are governed by Rule 144 of the SEC code. The rule severely limits the sale of lettered insider stock for three years following an initial underwriting. Of course, the rule doesn't apply to shares donated to a third party, like a religious group. In each case, shortly after Mayer transferred his stock to a yeshiva in Brooklyn, the restrictive legends on the stock were removed."

"How are the legends removed?"

"A letter from the shareholder requesting removal of the legends is sent to the company's attorney. The attorney then renders an opinion as to the legality of the requested transaction."

"And, of course, the attorney who rendered the opinion was Mark Federman?"

Max nodded. "That's right. And a short time after the legends were removed and new stock certificates issued, the shares of NovoMed surged."

McClure abruptly raised his hand. "Don't tell me. Soon after a run up in the shares, the yeshiva sold its NovoMed stock."

"Right again!"

"I recall you said that you had asked Federman to render an opinion on the legality of the yeshiva selling the donated shares."

"I did, but his reply was the same. It's perfectly legal for an insider to donate stock to a third party and for the third party, without recourse, to sell any of their shares whenever they choose."

Running his hand across the back of his neck, McClure gazed at the stack of NovoMed financial documents on the conference table. "I have a feeling, if we dig deep enough, we'll find much more revealing information buried in your company's financial documents."

# CHAPTER 15

Twenty-six years earlier, Holocaust survivor Eva Rubin sat on the edge of a high stool over a kitchen work table preparing loaves of braided challah dough for the Friday night Sabbath dinner.

Eva, a petite woman with white skin and captivating cobalt blue eyes she'd inherited her mother, was the sole survivor of a prominent German Jewish banking family. She had lost all her relatives in the Holocaust..

When the war ended, she met another Holocaust survivor, Isaac Rubin, at a DP camp in Germany. Drawn to each other, they soon married and emigrated to the Crown Heights section of Brooklyn, NY. Determined to build a new life, they started a dry cleaning business and raised three children. In honor of Eva's deceased father, the Rubins named their youngest son Mayer. Born on July 7, 1946, he was, according to Jewish law, circumcised eight days later in their local synagogue by a mohel.

A colicky, often sickly child, Mayer was, from an early age, prone to temper tantrums. Unlike his older brother and younger sister, he often disregarded or circumvented his mother's instructions. Despite his contentious behavior, however, he generally received no more than a reprimand from her.

On a fall day, in his senior year in high school, Mayer arrived home from school early. Standing in the doorway of the kitchen, he announced, as he had on countless days before, "I'm home."

He expected a warm response, but uncharacteristically, his mother ignored him and continued working. He was about to ask if he'd done something to displease her, but before he could, she put down the dough in her hand and fixed her blue eyes on him. "Your father is waiting for you in his study."

The angry tone of his mother's voice frightened Mayer. Lowering his eyes, he turned and retreated down a long corridor lined with books and Judaic artwork.

At the end of the corridor, he found his father in his study sitting at a large oak desk writing in a journal.

Pen in hand, Isaac Rubin looked up and glared at Mayer.

"This morning I had a disturbing meeting with the principal of your school. He told me your poor grades will prevent you from graduating with the rest of your class in June."

As Mayer prepared to respond, his father abruptly sprang from his chair and angrily warned, "Don't say a word. Sit down and listen to me carefully. Your mother and I have suffered a great deal. We've have been through more than you can imagine. As parents, our greatest hope is to see our children grow up well educated, have a steady income, and raise a family."

Mayer, his heart racing, listened in silence.

"I've never told you how I survived the concentration camps." Rolling up his left shirtsleeve, he pointed to the numbers tattooed on his forearm. "You see, this is what the Nazis did to me."

Mayer stared at the tattoo on his father's arm.

"First they took everything we owned and forced us to live in a filthy overcrowded ghetto. Then they shipped us in cattle cars to Auschwitz. By some miracle, they needed a skilled tailor. So instead of sending me to the gas chambers like the rest of my family, they gave me a sewing machine to make uniforms for SS officers. A day before the Russians overran Auschwitz, the Germans prodded us into boxcars and shipped us to Buchenwald. Again, I was lucky. The war ended before the Nazis could kill me."

Stunned, Mayer sat motionless.

"I still remember the day, April 11, 1945. An American tank rammed through the electrified barbed wire fence surrounding the camp and came to an abrupt stop in front of our barracks. The soldiers on the tank, rifles pointing in our direction, stared at us in disbelief until they realized we weren't German soldiers. I must have passed out because, when I awoke, I found myself in a bed with white linen sheets. The American soldiers had taken me to an Army hospital. God had granted me a second chance.

"A few months later, I met your mother in a refugee camp. She has blessed me with three children. Both your brother and sister are excellent students and have given us much joy, but you Mayer," he said, shaking his head, "all you've given your parents is grief."

Mayer, his face paling, began to perspire. Avoiding his father's gaze, he lowered his eyes and stared at the carpet. Then, slowly raising his head, in a faltering voice he addressed his father. "I'm sorry."

In an angry tone, Isaac Rubin lashed out at his son. "You're sorry? That's not good enough," he said, shaking his index finger at Mayer. "Fortunate for you, the principal of your school and I grew up in the same town in Poland and were close friends. As a personal favor to me, he's agreed to enroll you in a special program. It'll require diligent study on your part, but if you succeed, you'll graduate on time with the rest of your class. This is your last chance."

Relieved, Mayer regained his composure. "I promise. I won't disappoint you."

Isaac gazed at his son skeptically. "It's up to you now. I don't want to have this discussion with you ever again. Is that clear?"

"Yes," Mayer affirmed, nodding.

Later in the evening, Mayer stared at a picture of a white billowy cloud he had taped to the ceiling of his bedroom and reflected on his father's words. *As his father's son, he, too, had a special relationship with God that would serve him well throughout his life.*

# CHAPTER 16

Two years later, in the early winter of 1967, 19-year-old Mayer Rubin, recently employed at the brokerage firm of Sterling Securities, met a young Hasidic stockbroker, Aaron Weiss.

"Tell me, Mayer," Weiss said, wiping a sliver of chicken from his beard with a paper napkin,"Do you understand the biblical meaning of being a Jew?"

Drawing a pained breath, Mayer Rubin confided, "My knowledge of Jewish history and law is limited."

The next day Weiss delivered a stack of books to Mayer. Stimulated by the subject matter, he often found himself waking the next morning still clutching a book in his hands.

The biblical stories of Moses ascending Mt. Sinai to receive the Ten Commandments from God, King David's conquest of the Canaanites, his establishment of Jerusalem as the capital of Israel, and his son Solomon who built the first grand temple to house the Ark of the Covenant, all inspired Mayer, but one well-worn book would change his life.

The book, which he twice read, dealt with the life and mystical philosophies of Rabbi Israel Baal Shem Tov, referred to as the Besht. In 1736, he founded the modern Hasidic movement in the Carpathian Mountains of Eastern Europe. From a humble background shrouded in mystery, Baal Shem Tov created a new Kabalistic spiritualism for impoverished Jews living in Eastern Europe.

As Mayer's friendship with Weiss grew, so did the direction of their discussions. Several weeks later, he invited Mayer to meet his rebbe and participate in a Friday Shabbat (Sabbath) service.

Hasidim, Mayer discovered, used the term "rebbe" to describe the leader of their congregation, who also served as their spiritual advisor and mentor. They believe the rebbe possesses a special relationship with God and often consult him on matters of health and spirituality, as well as business decisions.

Rebbe Solomon Halberstram of the Bobov congregation based in Boro Park, Brooklyn took a liking to the outsider and encouraged Mayer to join their weekly Friday evening and Saturday morning services.

Impressed with Mayer's level of interest, the rebbe requested ha he stay after the Friday evening Tisch (meal) had ended. After all of the other men in the congregation had departed, from a corner of the empty shul, a voice called out to him. "Mayer, come and join me."

Uneasy, Mayer walked to the front of the sparse room and stared at the white-bearded figure sitting at a heavy wooden table. "Is something wrong?" he asked, his voice trembling.

"No, I just want to talk to you. Please sit down." Placing a cube of sugar into his mouth, the rebbe sipped tea from a large glass. "I'm pleased with your interest in our congregation, but I'm also concerned. Unlike most Jews who practice their faith when it's convenient, our lives are always entwined with God. His presence is with us everywhere, every moment of our humble existence. My advice, before you commit to our lifestyle, is to first spend time at our yeshiva in Israel."

Surprised, Mayer replied, "Israel? Why can't I learn what I need to know in Boro Park?"

The rebbe gazed at Mayer for several seconds, then said in a fatherly tone, "You could probably learn a lot, but learning is not the same as feeling and experiencing first-hand. That can only come from growing up in a Hasidic family."

The rebbe took another sip of tea and set the glass down. "Since you didn't grow up in a Hasidic family, the experience of living and working in Israel at our yeshiva will provide you with an understanding of what it is to be a Hasidic Jew. Mingle with our people, study the Torah, and learn the true roots of Judaism. When you return in a year or so and are still interested and committed, then I'll welcome you into our congregation with open arms."

Mayer contemplated the rebbe's advice for a week before requesting a meeting with his boss.

"Something with your job bothering you?" his boss asked.

"No. I like my job, but I need a change."

"Oh, sure, take a vacation," the manager fired back. "You'll come back refreshed."

Mayer shook his head. "No, that's not what I mean. I've decided I want to live in Israel for a while. I'll be leaving in two weeks."

Sensing Mayer had already made his decision, his boss replied stoically, "I'm sorry you're leaving, but I wish you good luck. Be careful. Israel is a dangerous place to live."

"Don't worry," Mayer said smugly, "I'm sure I'll be well protected."

# CHAPTER 17

Ten days later, over the intercom system of a Boeing 707 jet aircraft destined for Tel Aviv, an El Al flight attendant announced in English, then repeated in Hebrew and Yiddish, "The aircraft has been cleared for takeoff. Please be sure your seat belts are securely fastened."

Two minutes later, its engines at full power, the aircraft thrust down the long runway and up into the sky over Long Island. Amazed, Mayer peered through the window adjacent to his seat at the myriad of houses and scrambled highways below.

The 5,678-mile flight from JFK to David Ben-Gurion International Airport on the outskirts of Tel Aviv, almost full to capacity, spanned 11 hours. Two kosher meals were served, but feeling anxious, Mayer ate little, preferring instead to browse magazines and sleep.

Two hundred miles from Tel Aviv, the aircraft intercom crackled. A moment later a flight attendant announced, "In preparation for landing, all passengers must immediately return to their seats and securely fasten their seat belts."

A rush of anticipation gripped Mayer as the aircraft landed, taxied, and came to a stop 300 feet from the main terminal. Moments after the engines shut down, he grabbed his travel bag and moved to a side door. When the door opened, he descended a mobile staircase the ground crew had rolled out to meet the aircraft. As he walked to the terminal, he noted several Israeli soldiers carrying Uzi submachine guns.

Mayer collected his luggage and proceeded to customs inspection. Sitting behind a glass enclosure, a uniformed female agent requested his passport. He handed it to her, and she examined the unmarked pages.

"Is this your first visit to Israel?" she asked curtly.

Mayer nodded. "Yes."

"And what's the purpose of your visit?"

"To study and visit with relatives."

The agent stamped Mayer's passport, handed it back to him, and called for the next person in the line to step forward.

The airport, monitored by heavily armed soldiers, bustled with hundreds of multinational travelers carrying an array of suitcases, boxes, and canvas duffle bags.

Outside the customs gate a thin, bearded young man dressed in black trousers, a black vest, an open collar white shirt, with and a black yarmulke on his head approached Mayer. He'd been watching him pass through customs.

"Mayer Rubin?" the man said.

Startled, Mayer replied, "Yes."

"I'm Yossi Abramowitz. We've been expecting you. How was the trip?"

Mayer scanned the face of the figure standing in front of him. Reassured by what he saw, he said, "Okay, but it was a long flight."

Yossi smiled and reached for Mayer's suitcase. "Flying takes its toll on the body. You'll be fine in a few days."

Parked in front of the terminal, its engine running and a driver behind the wheel, was an aged jeep. Yossi tossed Mayer's suitcase onto the front passenger seat next to the driver and said, "You'll ride with me in the back. We're going to an Agudat Israel settlement. There you can rest. In a few days I'll take you to our yeshiva at Kiryat Bobov."

# CHAPTER 18

M cClure fixed his gaze on Max and asked, "What do you know about Mark Federman?"

Leaning back, Max gripped the armrest of his chair. "The first time I met him was at a meeting to discuss the private placement memo he had drafted. He was prematurely graying and wore wire-framed glasses that made him look older than he was. After the meeting, I decided it would be prudent to run a background check on him."

"What did you find?"

"Federman is a graduate of Columbia Law School, Phi Beta Kappa, a Kent Scholar, and a member of law review. After graduating from law school, he joined Neufeld, Cooper, and Weiss, a prominent New York law firm specializing in corporate and securities law. Nine years later, he resigned and formed his own firm."

"Was he a partner when he resigned from Neufeld?"

"I don't think so. Maybe that's why he started his own firm."

McClure scoffed. "I suspect, with his strong academic credentials, something about his performance or character hurt his chances of becoming a partner. We'll check into it. In the meantime, what else can you tell me about him?"

Rising from his chair, Max poured a cup of coffee and returned to the conference table. "Like Mayer, Federman is an Orthodox Jew, but you'd be hard pressed to know it from the way he dresses. Whenever we met, he was wearing a business suit."

McClure nodded and jotted a note on his pad. "Before I forget, did you bring the photographs of Mayer and his crew?"

Max pulled out a glassine envelope from his briefcase and passed it to McClure.

McClure eyed the photographs. "Who's the person on the left?"

"That's Mayer."

"And next to him?"

"Mark Federman."

"You're right. He looks like any typical business executive."

"A year after I joined NovoMed, I learned that he's a Talmudic scholar."

"What's a Talmudic scholar?"

Max thought for a moment. "Simply defined, a Talmudic scholar is an individual who has studied and mastered the complex oral interpretation of the written Hebrew Bible, the Torah. In Orthodox Judaism, the Talmud is the basis of religious authority. Federman also authored a definitive book on interpreting the Talmud."

"Seems like quite a studious guy."

"I guess so. He once told me he spends most of his free time studying Talmudic law."

McClure reached for a folder on the conference table marked "NovoMed Private Placement", opened the cover, and scanned the index page. Then he thumbed to a page that listed the names and addresses of subscribers. Pointing to the list, he asked, "Do you know any of the people or organizations on this list?"

Uneasy, Max winced. "I'm embarrassed to tell you . . . I don't know any of them. I do recall, however, before agreeing to join the company, having a discussion with Mark Federman. He assured me that all of the people, organizations, and yeshivas listed as subscribers were qualified investors."

As McClure prepared to ask another question, Velma buzzed him on the intercom.

"Mr. Jones is on the phone."

McClure pressed the speaker button. "Hello, Bob. Max Eisen is with me. Go ahead."

"I'm glad you're together," Jones replied. "I've got important information to share with you both."

# CHAPTER 19

C olumns of soldiers and military trucks slowed traffic to a trickle along the road leading to the Agudat Israel settlement. Unaccustomed to the intense sun, Mayer wiped the perspiration from his brow with a handkerchief. Turning to Yossi, he asked, "What's going on?"

Yossi smiled. "The Arabs are threatening to attack us, so the army is preparing, just in case."

Soon after they arrived at the settlement, Yossi introduced Mayer to a group of young Hasidic men who had recently emigrated from Eastern Europe. Each man carried a rifle slung over his shoulder. Though the sight of Hasidic men carrying rifles frightened Mayer, he remained silent.

"Get some rest. I'll be back in a few days," Yossi said as he departed.

Mayer welcomed Yossi's suggestion. The long trip had tired him. Feeling light-headed after a glass of wine at dinner, he returned to his room, undressed, and fell into a deep sleep.

At 6:30 a.m., an elderly Hasidic man wearing his prayer shawl awakened Mayer. "Get up," he shouted. "The war has started. We need to get ready."

Confused, Mayer jumped out of bed and scrambled for his clothes. Outside, he could hear sporadic gunfire and loud explosions. Ironically, he had arrived in Israel a day before the Six Day Israeli-Arab War began. Unaccustomed to gunfire, he was terrified by the thought of being wounded or, even worse, killed.

Aided by Russian advisors, the Syrians, in alliance with Jordan and Egypt had launched multi-directional attacks on Israel. Overly confident, the Egyptians prematurely issued a postage stamp to commemorate their anticipated victory.

On the first evening of the war, armed Palestinian militia, known as Fedayeen, cut their way through a section of the settlement's barbed wire fence and killed two sentries guarding a dormitory housing young women and children. Unable to reach the sentries' mobile radio, the settlement leader, a tough, stocky, red-bearded Russian, accompanied by 12 armed men, cautiously approached the dormitory.

They found the bodies of the two young sentries, their throats slashed, in a pool of blood in front of the dormitory. Not hearing any sounds within the dormitory, they feared the worst, but were unprepared for the carnage they found. All the young women had been raped, strangled, and mutilated with knives. The young children, their bodies lined up in a row in front of the women's corpses, had been shot in the back of head. To avoid detection, the Fedayeen infiltrators had attached silencers to their weapons.

Strictly adhering to Jewish law requiring every part of a deceased person's body be collected before burial, the settlement leader requested that Mayer assist the burial team. Unfamiliar with death, Mayer passed out several times while he collected body parts. For days after, he had little appetite for food and slept poorly. *How could this happen?* he asked himself.

A young rabbi, his deep-set brown eyes reflecting the weight of his own personal grief, counseled Mayer, "This is the nature of Jewish life in Israel and the reason we can't retreat. If we turn our backs, we'll all die as our people did in the Holocaust. Whatever the price, we must never allow it to happen again. God will protect us."

Later in the afternoon, a squad of IDF soldiers arrived to provide security for the settlement. The same Fedayeen who had breached the barbed wire fence the night before attempted to infiltrate the settlement again, but this time the Israeli soldiers waited to spring a trap. Equipped with night vision binoculars, they observed the Arab infiltrators cutting through the fence. When all of the infiltrators were within the perimeter, the Israeli lieutenant gave the signal to open fire. Within two minutes, all of the infiltrators fell to the ground.

Spotting one of infiltrators desperate to exit through a hole in the fence, the lieutenant fired his rifle. Approaching the breached fence, the soldiers found all of the Fedayeen lying face down on the ground with the exception of the lone soldier who had attempted to flee. The lieutenant's single bullet had found its mark.

By the end of the short 1967 Six-Day War, Israel's borders had dramatically changed. The Golan Heights, East Jerusalem, the West Bank, Gaza Strip, and the Sinai Peninsula were now under Israeli control.

When Yossi Abramowitz returned to the settlement one week after the war ended, he found
Mayer eating breakfast in the communal
dining room.

"So, Mayer, how do you like Israel?"

For a moment Mayer stared at Yossi. "I've had an amazing
experience. Imagine, on my first trip to Israel, a war breaks
out. Unbelievable!"

Yossi smiled stoically. "Well, my friend. In Israel, we're
always in a state of war. You'll get used to it."

"Get used to war?" Mayer fired back. "How do you get
used to war?"

Yossi shrugged. "Actually, you don't ever get used to war.
You just learn to live with it."

Yossi's comment frightened Mayer, but he tried to keep
his composure.

Noting the distressed look on Mayer's face, Yossi placed his arm over his shoulder. "Don't worry. You'll be fine. The roads are open again, so we can safely drive to Bat Yam. Rabbi Nussbaum, the director of the Kiryat Bobov Yeshiva, is expecting us. We should get going. I'll wait outside while you pack your bag."

Fifteen minutes later, with Mayer sitting next to Yossi in the back seat, the driver shifted rapidly into third gear and headed the jeep south along the coastal highway en route to their destination at Bat Yam, a suburb of Tel Aviv.

The Hasidic yeshiva study center at Kiryat Bobov, established by Rebbe Halberstram in 1958, was comprised of a series of drab, non-descript buildings. Within the yeshiva complex, situated on a bluff offering a spectacular view of the Mediterranean, students studied, prayed, received their meals, and slept. For the next 14 months, Kiryat Bobov would serve as Mayer's home.

As the jeep neared the Bobov Yeshiva, the main gate swung open. In the courtyard, an elderly man with a long white beard dressed in black Hasidic attire waved and called out, "Shalom, Yossi."

"Shalom," Yossi replied as he and Mayer approached the rabbi. "I'd like you to meet Mayer Rubin."

Rabbi Nussbaum locked his dark eyes on Mayer. "Welcome to Kiryat Bobov."

Though Mayer recognized the Eastern European inflection in the rabbi's faltering English, he remained silent.

"We've been expecting you. I hope your trip went well."

Feigning a smile, Mayer replied, "Yes, it did."

The rabbi nodded. He then turned his eyes to Yossi Abramowitz. "Will you be joining us for dinner?"

"No, but I'll be back in a day or so. In the meantime, I'm leaving Mayer in your care. Shalom."

When Yossi's jeep had passed from view, the rabbi turned to Mayer. "Yossi is one of our brightest young men. You can learn a lot from him."

Mayer nodded, but didn't comment. Suitcase in hand, he followed the rabbi into the yeshiva compound down a narrow corridor leading to his private study. Rabbi Nussbaum lowering into a black leather chair behind a large wooden desk, then motioned for Mayer to sit in one of the chairs in front of his desk.

"I understand you were raised in a Jewish family, but your parents are not Hasidim?"

Mayer's face flushed. "That is true, but they're Holocaust survivors."

Unexpectedly, the rabbi sprang from his chair. Visibly agitated, he stood in front of Mayer, rolled up his shirtsleeve, and pointed to the numbers tattooed on his left forearm. "I too, am a Holocaust survivor," he said in an angry tone. "The Nazis thought they could kill us all, but they were wrong. God saved us. We've committed ourselves to never let it happen again."

After he pulled down his shirtsleeve, the rabbi returned to his desk and gazed at Mayer. "Now tell me . . . why do you want to live your life as a Hasid?"

Mayer lowered his eyes and pretended he was pondering the rabbi's question. Several seconds passed before he raised his head and gazed at the rabbi. "I believe being a member of the Hasidic community will bring me closer to God."

"You understand our beliefs and customs set us apart from other Jews?"

"Yes, but I welcome the opportunity to prove myself."

"You know, you're taking on a heavy burden."

"I understand."

The rabbi nodded approvingly. "Then we welcome you. My daughter Rachel will show you to your room. Tomorrow your study program will begin. Tonight we eat at six-thirty. I'll see you then. Shalom."

# CHAPTER 21

J ones pressed the phone to his ear. "Before I tell you what we've uncovered, I think you should know—whoever is responsible for installing the bugs in Max's offices are professionals. My guess is the bugs were manufactured in the Czech Republic. They transmit on a radio frequency seldom used in the United States, and to conserve power, operate only when an audible sound level is detected."

Darting McClure a wide-eyed glance, Max moved closer to the conference table speakerphone. "I understand you found another bug after I left my office Tuesday night."

"Yes. In addition to the one removed from your office, we found another hidden in the light fixture hanging over your conference room table. A transmitter concealed under the ceiling tiles is connected to an antenna cleverly disguised as part of the communication equipment mounted on the roof. It's designed to transmit signals within a radius of twenty-five miles."

"Do you know how long they've been in my offices?"

"Hard to say for sure, but the adhesive holding the bugs in place are somewhat yellow. That would indicate they were installed some time ago."

"Damn! That's probably how they got hold of confidential information."

McClure nodded and leaned into the speakerphone. "Have you located the site they're transmitting to?"

"Yes, we've tracked the monitoring station to the basement of a two-family house in Teaneck, New Jersey."

"That's not far from my office."

"That's right, Max. Our surveillance team has observed a lot of activity in the house. Groups of four to five men wearing long black coats and large black hats meet three, sometimes four times a week in the basement. They usually stay several hours before leaving in pairs. On other occasions, we've seen similarly dressed men arrive, then depart a short time later carrying what appear to be heavy leather travel bags. What we haven't yet figured out is what they're carrying in those bags."

McClure jumped in. "Did you get their license plate numbers?"

"Oh yes, and we're running a check. We've also determined that the house is owned by a Hasidic family now in Israel on an extended visit."

Max, his hand covering his mouth, stared at the speakerphone in silence.

"What's the next step?" McClure asked.

"We've set up a remote monitoring station to capture all telephone communications. We're also monitoring conversations within the house with a parabolic microphone. If we need them, the bugs we removed from Max's office will be useful for transmitting fake information."

"Anything else?"

"No, Harry. That's it for now."

McClure stood up, stretched his arms behind his neck, and gazed through one of the tall windows facing the courtyard. For a moment, his eyes followed his Basenji, Aristotle, chasing a butterfly in the garden below. Turning from the window, he faced Max and noted the dejected look on his face. "I know the discovery of the bugs in your office has upset you, but look at it this way. Now that we've located the bugs, we have tangible evidence that someone is sabotaging your company."

Max pursed his lips. "You're right. I'm just feeling a little pissed off at myself."

"I understand. Look, it's after six. What do you say we continue our discussion over a hot corned beef sandwich and a few beers?"

Max gave a faint smile. "Good idea. I need a break, but first, where's the men's room?"

"Follow me."

# CHAPTER 22

M ayer was assigned to a single room in the yeshiva's dormitory wing. Each morning, except on the Sabbath and holidays, he followed a strict Judaic ritual. Upon awakening, he bathed, put on tefillin, and prayed.

A symbolic reminder of a Jew's devotion to God's commandments, tefillin consist of a black leather box wrapped around a man's arm with leather straps and a second black leather box positioned on the forehead. Tefillin boxes contain four sections of the Five Books of the Hebrew Bible, (Exodus 13:1-10, 13:11-16 and Deuteronomy 6:4-9, 11:13-21) written in Hebrew on parchment made from the skin of a kosher animal.

His morning prayers completed, Mayer walked through a long narrow corridor connecting his dormitory to the main yeshiva building and joined fellow students for breakfast in the communal dining room.

From 9 a.m., until noon each weekday, he studied the Torah with other yeshiva students. In the afternoon, following a short lunch break, he joined a class devoted to Jewish law (Halakhah), the 613 commandments (Mitzvot) handed down by Moses governing every aspect of an Orthodox Jew's life.

To enhance Mayer's proficiency in Yiddish and reading Hebrew text, Rabbi Nussbaum provided a special tutor. Every afternoon at 3:30, he met with a bearded, soft-spoken, elderly man, Lev Stern.

At their first meeting, Stern offered Mayer an insight into his own life. "I'm the last member of a large Lithuanian family to survive the Holocaust. There's little time left for me, so it's important for you and other young Jewish men to keep our heritage and traditions alive and carry them into the future."

Pursing his lips angrily, Stern waved his index finger into the air. "Language has its own unique meanings. For Jews, Yiddish expresses the soul of our people, but thanks to that gonif, Eliezer Ben-Yehuda, the Israeli government would like us all to speak Hebrew. It's an affront to God.

"Hebrew is for reading the Torah, but in the Hasidic community, communication is dependent on your ability to read, write, and speak Yiddish."

With the prodding of his teacher, Mayer progressed rapidly. Impatient, two months into his studies, he asked his teacher, "When will I know I've mastered Yiddish?"

Lev Stern smiled with his eyes. "When you think in Yiddish, then you've arrived, and my job is over." Unlike his earlier high school years, Mayer felt motivated to keep up with his studies.

Ten weeks later, Rabbi Nussbaum summoned Mayer to his office. Arriving early, he found the door to the rabbi's office partially ajar. Mayer peered through a crack between the doorframe and the hinged side of the door, and silently observed the rabbi in a heightened state of prayer.

While he recited from a prayer book held in his right hand, the rabbi bent his knees and rocked his body back and forth rhythmically. As he prayed, the rapidly increasing rocking momentum of his body contorted his facial expression. He appeared to be in a hypnotic state over which he had no control. Suddenly his rapid jerking body movements stopped. His facial expression returned to normal, and he stood erect and motionless. Retrieving a handkerchief from his trouser pocket, he wiped the perspiration from his forehead and returned to his desk.

Mayer remained silent and reveled in the voyeuristic experience. A minute later, pretending he'd just arrived, he announced his presence, "Shalom, Rabbi."

Caught off guard, the rabbi took a moment to focus on the figure in the doorway. "Shalom. You startled me. Please come in and sit down." As Mayer slipped into a wooden chair, the rabbi said, "I've heard you're doing well in your studies."

Mayer smiled through his full beard and replied in Yiddish, "Thank you. I've learned a great deal."

The rabbi nodded. "Yes, I can tell your command of Yiddish has greatly improved. Now it's time for you to visit the Holy City of Jerusalem. I've made arrangements for you to stay with Rabbi Katz."

"When do I leave?" Mayer asked anxiously.

"Tomorrow morning. You'll be picked up at seven. Be ready."

# CHAPTER 23

Eager to get underway, by 6:30 a.m., Mayer had dressed, prayed, and packed his travel bag. As he walked down the long dimly lit corridor connecting the compound dormitories with the main yeshiva buildings, he glanced at his watch. Deciding he had time to indulge in a quick breakfast, he dropped his travel bag near the front door of the communal dining room and headed to the cafeteria line. As he searched for a table, a voice called out to him.

"Shalom, Mayer."

A surprised look on his face, Mayer turned and greeted Yossi Abramowitz. "Shalom. You're up early."

Yossi nodded. "When you're ready, we'll leave."

At five minutes before seven, Mayer grabbed his travel bag and joined Yossi. The same mud-spattered green jeep, canvas top down, he rode in when he first arrived in Israel was waiting. It was a clear, warm morning, and Mayer hopped into the rear seat next to Yossi. As the jeep got underway, Mayer noticed a gun on the floor below Yossi's seat and another in the space between the driver and passenger seat.

"Don't worry," Yossi said, sensing Mayer's uneasiness. "It's only a precaution—in case we run into any trouble."

Soon after they passed several burned out cars and trucks, vestiges of the short-lived Arab-Israeli Six-Day War, Yossi turned to Mayer. "It's important for you to remember, Solomon's Temple, which once stood on the Temple Mount, had been the home of the Holy of the Holiest. Now that Jerusalem has been recaptured, one day the Temple will be rebuilt, the Ark of the Covenant returned to its rightful place on the Temple Mount, and all the lands God promised to our ancestors returned to the Jewish people."

# CHAPTER 24

McClure, with Max following, maneuvered into the crowded Carnegie Deli toward a young dark-haired woman registering the names of customers awaiting tables. Turning her head in his direction, she greeted McClure curtly. "There're a wait of thirty to forty-five minutes. What's—"

Before she completed the sentence, a stocky waiter sporting a white broom mustache took hold of McClure's arm and reproached the young woman. "I'll take care of Mr. McClure. Gentlemen, follow me." Stopping at a corner table surrounded by framed photographs of prominent movie personalities and politicians, he said, "I trust this table is okay, Mr. McClure?"

McClure nodded his approval and said, "What's all the activity tonight, Oscar?"

"It's always a madhouse when there's a concert at Carnegie Hall. An hour from now we'll be deserted. So, what can I get for you gentlemen?" Their orders quickly jotted on his notepad, the waiter nodded and collected the menus.

Forty minutes later, satiated by overstuffed corned beef sandwiches washed down with glasses of Bass Ale, McClure viewed Max's empty plate. "Feeling better?"

"Yeah, I guess I was hungry, but I'm still upset over the damn bugs your men found in my office. Do you think there's a connection between Mayer Rubin and the fluctuation in our stock?"

"There could be a link, so I've asked an old friend, Stan Jacob, to review your financial statements. He's a highly regarded SEC attorney with an uncanny knack for spotting financial irregularities the average person would overlook. I've given him your number, so you can expect a call. Be candid and give any information he requests."

"Gentlemen, can I get you anything else?" the waiter asked.

"Coffee for me," McClure replied.

"And you, sir?"

"The same."

The waiter returned with two white mugs of coffee and placed the check on McClure's side of the table. "Take your time, gentlemen. There's no hurry at this hour."

Reaching across the table, Max grabbed the check. "This one is on me."

McClure smiled graciously. "Okay, I surrender." He raised his coffee cup to his mouth, took a sip, then said, "I've been meaning to ask you. Whatever happened to the inventor, Dr. Darmin?"

"That's another story. About two years ago, on his way to a board meeting, Darmin's car collided with a trailer truck and he was killed. The strange thing is, I thought Mayer, being so religious, would be upset, but he wasn't. In fact, after Dr. Darmin's funeral, he never mentioned him again."

Greeted by unusually mild spring weather as they exited onto Seventh Avenue, McClure suggested they walk to the garage where Max had parked. As they sauntered east on 54th Street, McClure turned to Max. "Earlier today you mentioned your assistant wasn't surprised when you told her Mayer Rubin was indicted."

"Yes, that's right."

"But wasn't there something else she wanted to tell you?"

Max smiled. "Yes. The next day she came into my office. A serious look on her face, she closed the door and sat in front of my desk. 'Well,' she began, 'every time there's a board meeting, Mr. Rubin gets a little out of hand.' I asked what she meant by out of hand. Uncharacteristically, Beth blushed. Then she told me that, before the board met, she would bring Mayer coffee in the special kosher cups reserved for him. On several occasions, as she placed his coffee cup on the conference table, he would slip his hand under her dress and grope her 'derriere.' "

McClure shook his head. "What a guy."

"There's more, Harry. She said, 'since it wasn't the first time, she did something she probably shouldn't have done.' When I asked what it was, she said, 'you know how fussy he was about eating or drinking on special kosher dishes.' I nodded."

Holding back a smile, McClure asked, "What did she do?"

"At the next board meeting, when Mayer arrived, she seated him in the conference room. As usual, he asked for coffee. When she returned, unbeknownst to him, she had poured his coffee into a regular cup. Obviously, it wasn't kosher. This time she stayed on the other side of the conference room table so he couldn't touch her." Max rolled his eyes. "The funny thing . . . he never knew she switched the cups."

McClure couldn't resist the opportunity to poke fun at Max. "Do all of your directors behave that way?"

Caught off guard, Max replied defensively, "That kind of behavior is totally unacceptable and . . ."

Grinning, McClure asked, "Is that so?"

Suddenly aware he was the beneficiary of McClure's ribbing, Max shook his head and smiled. As they continued up Park Avenue, both men broke into laughter.

In front of Max's garage, McClure extended his hand. "I'll be in Washington tomorrow, but I'll be in touch. If you need to reach me, call Velma. And say hello to Katherine."

"I will, Harry. Good night."

McClure withdrew a cigar from his suit pocket. Cutting the end with a cigar cutter, he lit it with a wooden match and inhaled. A light rain had earlier watered the tiny sprouting buds of Ginkgo trees lining the streets of New York's midtown. In another month, their branches would support unique fan-like leaves. *How incredible these graceful prehistoric trees, miraculous survivors of the ice age, continue to thrive in New York's automobile-polluted environment.*

As he drifted back to his brownstone, he puffed on his cigar and mulled over the information Jones had gathered on Mayer Rubin. Though not yet certain Mayer Rubin was the M. Rubin Davidov was seeking, nevertheless he sensed that Mayer Rubin was somehow linked to whoever was undermining Max's company. *My dilemma*, he thought. *How do I help Max without compromising my assignment for Ari? Should be interesting, Harry.*

# CHAPTER 25

Mayer's jeep encountered a series of sandbagged checkpoints along the 35 mile dusty highway from Bat Yam to Jerusalem. At each of the heavily fortified checkpoints, the driver retrieved a card from his breast pocket and presented it to an armed Israeli soldier. After an exchange of a few words in Hebrew, the barrier blocking the road lifted and the jeep continued until the next checkpoint.

Along the route, the jeep passed long convoys of empty army trucks returning from Jerusalem heading back to Haifa for food and supplies desperately needed by beleaguered Jews living in Jerusalem.

The jeep entered the city from the west and passed the final checkpoints before it arrived at its destination. Built into the side of a hill, the multi-building enclave of Rabbi Jacob Katz served as his home and yeshiva study center.

Yossi sprang from the jeep and pointed to the expanse of houses along the side of the hill. "During the British colonial rule of Jerusalem from 1917 to 1948, the English mandated a uniform building code requiring every new building façade be constructed of a local pinkish white limestone known as Jerusalem Stone. The stone has the unique characteristic of changing hue as the sun travels from east to west across the sky."

Fascinated by the unusual architecture, Mayer asked, "What are those pockmarks?"

Gazing up, Yossi replied, "Jordanian batteries regularly shelled this area until the Israeli army drove them out during the recent war."

Mayer nodded.

Yossi knocked on an imposing wooden door at the compound's main entrance. A minute later the door swung open and a fair-skinned girl greeted them in English.

"Please come in. My father is expecting you." Leading the way through a large living room furnished with dark furniture and an ornate Persian rug, she pointed to an open door leading to the courtyard.

In a shaded corner, a middle-aged, broad shouldered bearded rabbi sat reading a newspaper. Seeing the figures approach, he called out, "Yossi, please come in." Rising from his wicker chair, the rabbi warmly embraced Yossi. Turning his head, he then addressed Mayer. "You must be Mayer Rubin. Shalom."

Surprised by the rabbi's American accent, Mayer replied in a cautious tone, "Shalom, Rabbi. You speak like an American."

Rabbi Katz grinned. "Oh, yes, I speak American English. I grew up in Cleveland, Ohio, but I've been living in Israel since 1948." The rabbi motioned to a pitcher of iced tea on the table. "Please have some refreshment." He then turned to Yossi. "I need an hour of your time."

Clutching a tall glass of iced tea, Yossi replied, "I'll be back in the morning."

The rabbi nodded. "I'll see you then."

A moment after Yossi departed, Rabbi Katz turned to Mayer. Clasping his hands together, he asked, "How much do you know about Israel and its history?"

Embarrassed by the rabbi's question, Mayer gritted his teeth. "Only what I've read."

"I see. Then there is much for you to learn. Tomorrow, you'll be taken on a tour of Jerusalem. Until just a few weeks ago, the Old City, including the Western Wall and the Temple Mount, were in Muslim hands. Now Jerusalem is once again under Jewish control. Jews from all parts of the Diaspora will soon freely pray at the Wall."

Inspired by the impassioned tone of Rabbi Katz's voice, Mayer gingerly asked, "Do you think a new temple will be built on the Temple Mount?"

Leaning forward in his chair, Rabbi Katz, his eyes filled with passion, stared hypnotically at Mayer. "I can tell you

without reservation, there will be a day when the only building standing on the Temple Mount will be the sanctuary of
Yahweh."

# CHAPTER 26

The next morning, Yossi sat at a table in Rabbi Katz's living room sipping black coffee from a large white mug. Scanning the front page of *the Jerusalem Post,* his eyes were drawn to the headline "Jewish Leaders Condemn Dyan Temple Mount Decision. " As he read the article, he heard a familiar voice echo from the far side of the room.

"Shalom, Yossi."

Folding the newspaper, Yossi turned his head and called out to Mayer, "Shalom. Come and join me."

As Mayer lowered into a dark wooden chair, Yossi smiled and said, "You're in luck. Today you'll be getting the royal tour."

"What do you mean?" Mayer asked a puzzled look on his face.

"Rabbi Katz has asked Professor Avraham Taube to take you on a tour of Jerusalem. Not many people have that opportunity. He is, as you'll soon find out, an incredible man."

Not sure what he could expect, Mayer feigned a smile.

Yossi continued. "Professor Taube is one of a small number of Palestinian-born Jews who rose through the ranks and became officers in the British Army during the Second World War. His experience proved invaluable in 1948 when Israel, having declared its sovereignty, immediately found itself at war with Egypt, Jordan, and Syria. He retired from the army as a Colonel in 1955, and he is now a Professor of Archeology and History at Hebrew University in Jerusalem."

From the corner of his eye, Mayer caught the image of a figure striding toward their table.

Professor Taube was not the stereotype of a Sabra. Tall, fair skinned, and blue eyed, his streaked blond hair and light beard stood out in sharp contrast to the dark hair and beards of most Orthodox Jewish Israeli men. Dressed in a tan shirt rolled up at the sleeves, tan pants, an army-style fatigue hat and tan boots, he looked as though he'd just returned from an African safari.

As Professor Taube approached their table, Yossi stood and whispered to Mayer, "Don't worry. He's one of us."

"Shalom, Yossi."

Yossi smiled and shook Professor Taube's hand. "Shalom, Professor. Let me introduce you to Mayer Rubin. He's come from America to study our customs and heritage."

Taube turned to Mayer, a probing look in his intense blue eyes, and said, "If you're ready, we can leave now."

Shortly after Mayer and Taube departed, Yossi reopened the newspaper. Knowing the Temple Mount article would be a topic of discussion at his meeting with Rabbi Katz, he read it carefully.

M ax lifted the phone receiver to his ear. "I was hoping you'd call, Harry. Anything new?"

"I spoke with Jones earlier in the day. His men are monitoring the house in Teaneck, New Jersey. The only problem we've run into is that all the recorded discussions are in Yiddish."

Max chuckled. "I should have warned you. Among their own, the Hasidim converse in Yiddish."

"Fortunately, we've found a solution. The mother of one of my managers is a Holocaust survivor. She speaks and reads Yiddish and is translating the tapes on an ongoing basis."

"That's great," Max said, pressing the phone to his ear.

"Jones's surveillance has also uncovered another significant piece of the puzzle. It appears the group Mayer Rubin controls has interests in at least ten different companies, including your own. In the prospectus you filed with the SEC he's listed as a director of one of the companies."

"Which company?"

"Give me a minute," McClure said, as he thumbed through a manila folder. "Here it is. It's called Applied Medical Resources."

"Sure. I remember his mentioning that company."

"In several of the other companies like Hi-Tec Medical, he's listed only as a consultant."

"Of course. That's why, when we filed our prospectus with the SEC, he didn't have to disclose their names."

"Now, are you ready for another surprise?"

Max shot back, "You mean there's more?"

"You bet, a lot more. First, guess who the attorney of record is for all ten companies?"

"Don't tell me—Mark Federman!"

"You got it. They usually follow a similar scenario. First, they latch onto an early stage company with a good story to tell. Then they make certain the company, before going public, needs cash, which they readily supply in a private placement."

Max sighed. "Sounds familiar."

"The money is generated through Mayer's network of investors and yeshivas in Brooklyn. Yeshivas carry an IRS nonprofit designation, so minimal accounting records are maintained. We checked several of the yeshivas listed in your prospectus and cross-referenced them with the other companies in which both Mayer Rubin and Mark Federman have an interest. It turns out many of the yeshivas exist in name only. The address is often a private residence. By the way, Max, how is your stock holding up?"

"Not well. Every time it seems to recover, they unload another block of stock. The low stock price is discouraging potential investors. It closed yesterday at $4.25. At this point, it will be difficult to raise new capital without giving the company away."

I know you're having a tough time, Max, but think of all you've accomplished."

"Don't worry. I've invested too much of my life in NovoMed to cave in now."

"That's what I hoped you'd say. I'll be in touch in a few days."

Max hung up the phone, and then picked up a pencil and held it with both hands. As he stared at the NovoMed private placement document on his desk and reflected on McClure's revelations, he snapped the pencil in two.

# CHAPTER 28

Professor Taube motioned to a tan Land Rover parked diagonally across from Rabbi Katz's residence. "Hop in, Mayer. We're going to the heart of Jerusalem."

With his right hand anchored to the steering wheel, Taube glanced in Mayer's direction. "Jerusalem is a city with a long history. It's the spiritual center of the three great religions—Judaism, Christianity, and Islam. Each religion claims territorial rights, but around 1004 B.C.E., long before Islam or Christianity laid any claim to the holy city, King David captured Jerusalem from the Jebusites and established Jerusalem as the capital of his new Judaic Kingdom. Soon after his conquest, he began planning for a sacred temple." Pausing, Taube asked, "Am I going too fast?"

Mayer shook his head. "Oh, no, Professor, please continue."

"King David died before he could ultimately realize his dream of building a Grand Temple, but it was fulfilled by his son Solomon, who enhanced his father's building plans. Completed in 957 B.C.E, the Temple took seven years to build and stood on the Temple Mount over four hundred years before it was destroyed by the Babylonians."

Taube stopped the Land Rover at a checkpoint on the road leading into east Jerusalem. "ID," the Israeli soldier demanded in Hebrew. As he retrieved a card from his shirt pocket, a second soldier, clutching an Uzi submachine, eyed the behavior of the car's passenger. The soldier scanned the card, looked at Taube again, then saluted.

"Colonel, you need to be careful," he said as he returned the card to Taube. "Snipers are a constant threat in this area." Taube nodded and shifted the Land Rover into first gear.

As they approached Jerusalem, he turned to Mayer. "You're one of the first civilians to visit an area closed to Jews since 1948. That's when the Jordanians took over East Jerusalem. We won the war, but due to a biased United Nations resolution, the Jordanians ended up controlling the old city. Although we were promised access to the Western Wall, it was only a myth. The Jordanians totally restricted our access." Taube sneered. "Now all of Jerusalem is in Jewish hands, and that's where we want it to stay."

Near the closest entrance to the Western Wall, Taube parked the Land Rover alongside several army trucks guarded by Israeli soldiers. "From here we'll walk," he said, pointing to the arched entrance. "The architecture is characteristic of the Ottoman Turks who captured Jerusalem in 1517 and ruled for 400 years. You'll see it all over the Middle East.

"In 1917, however, near the end of World War I, the British army, led by General Allenby, re-captured Jerusalem. The English held on to Jerusalem until 1948, when Israel became a state. The gate we're about to enter is referred to as the Dung Gate."

An amused look on his face, Mayer asked, "Did you say Dung Gate?"

Taube smiled. "Yes, outside the Dung Gate, on the same ground we're standing, was the site of the Jerusalem dump. Animal intestines and droppings not permitted on the sacrificial altar in the Temple were brought here and burned. Now you know how the Dung Gate got its name."

Two hundred feet into the walled city, Taube stopped and retrieved a map from his knapsack. Stooping to the ground, he unfolded the map and placed it on the stone pavement. Extending his right arm, he pointed to a spot on the map, then gazed up at a weathered stone-wall rising to a height of sixty-five feet. "That," he said in a solemn tone, "is the most sacred Jewish ground on earth. A few hundred feet beyond the wall is the site where both Solomon's and Herod's Temples once stood."

Overwhelmed, Mayer wiped the perspiration from his brow. "So that's the Western Wall I've heard so much about."

Taube nodded. "It's the sole remaining wall of the second great temple built by King Herod. It's also, as our Christian and Muslim friends like to call it, the Wailing Wall. During the Ottoman Empire, Muslims called the Wall El-Make, or the "place of weeping." The name continued with the British occupation of Jerusalem. Since the recent Israeli capture of Jerusalem, Jews have returned to calling it the Western Wall."

Mayer stared at the Temple Mount intently, and then turned to Taube. "Can we get a little closer?"

"I think we can. Just be careful." In front of the Western Wall the Israeli Army had bulldozed many of the buildings constructed during the Jordanian occupation. Piles of debris remained.

Taube again pointed to the Temple Mount. "A few weeks ago, on the third day of the war, Israeli parachutists broke through the Lions' Gate and unfurled the Israeli flag on the Temple Mount. Before long, this area will be as it was before the Jordanians closed it off in 1948, packed with Jews praying at the wall."

"And what's the building on the other side of the wall?"

Taube sneered. "That's the most famous Muslim shrine in Jerusalem, second only to the Islamic shrine in Mecca, the Dome of the Rock. Muslims call it the Noble Sanctuary."

Mayer squinted through his glasses and studied the Dome. Looking puzzled, he turned to Taube. "I don't understand. How could a Muslim Holy shrine be on the ground where the Temple stood?"

"Good question. The Dome was built on the Temple Mount long after the first and second Temples were destroyed."

Mayer adjusted his glasses and looked at Taube. "I'm curious. Where was the Ark of the Covenant kept?"

Pleased by Mayer's interest, Taube replied, "The first temple built by Solomon contained within its walls an inner chamber specially designed as a sanctuary for the Ark of the Covenant. We know in 586 B.C.E, prior to the Babylonians looting and burning Solomon's Temple, the Ark and many of the temple's treasures disappeared. Five hundred years after the destruction of Solomon's Temple, Herod the Great built the second temple on the site of the first temple. Though pretending to be a Jew, in truth, Herod was no more than a puppet of the Romans."

Noting the intense sun had reddened Mayer's face, Taube reached into his knapsack and handed him a bottle of water. "Drink it. You'll feel better. Let's get out of the sun and take a break."

Mayer wiped his brow with a handkerchief, then drank the entire bottle of water. Refreshed, he looked at Taube. "I'd like to hear more."

"Between 687 and 691, the ninth Caliph Bad al-Mali commissioned the building of the Dome of the Rock on the Temple Mount. It's a shrine, not a place of worship. Muslims believe the rock, in the center of the dome, is the spot where

Muhammad ascended through the heavens to receive divine guidance from Allah."

Mayer pointed to another tall building on the Temple Mount and asked, "And what's that building?"

"Ah, that's where Muslims pray. It's called the al-Aqsa Mosque."

"Can we walk on the Temple Mount?"

Taube shook his head. "Unfortunately, at least for now, Jews are not permitted to enter the Temple Mount area."

Confused, Mayer frowned. "I don't understand. I thought we now occupy all of Jerusalem?"

"We do, but for some unexplained reason, days after the Israeli army occupied Jerusalem, Defense Secretary Moshe Dayan relinquished control of the Temple Mount to the Waqf Islamic Trust. For now, Jews aren't permitted to pray on the Mount."

Mayer's reddened face tightened. "That's outrageous. How could he restrict us from visiting the ground where our temples once stood?"

"We all agree it was a tragic mistake for Dayan to turn over control of the Temple Mount to the Muslims. For now, however, Israeli soldiers strictly enforce his orders." Taube inhaled, then added, "Be assured! It will change. Jews will retake the Temple Mount and drive all Muslims out, once and forever."

In the distance, they could hear the sound of gunfire. "The army is still cleaning up this area, so we must be careful.

Perhaps the next time you visit Israel, it will be safer." Taube glanced at his watch. "It's one-thirty. How about some lunch?"

Mayer smiled. "Yea, I'd like that."

"I know a great Hungarian restaurant not far from here. Let's go."

# CHAPTER 29

A rtur Zoltan, the owner/chef of Café Buda-Pesht, a
small restaurant situated on a side street of the
Jewish quarter of West Jerusalem, prided himself on
serving the finest kosher Hungarian cuisine in the Middle East.
A few minutes after Professor Taube and Mayer took seats at a
corner table in the café's open garden room, Taube gazed up
into the dark eyes of a large man sporting a grey handlebar
mustache and a white apron.

"Shalom, Avraham," the man said.

Taube returned the greeting and grasped the outstretched
hand of the friend with whom he had served in a predomi-
nantly Jewish unit of the British Army stationed in Egypt
during World War II. "This is a surprise. What brings you
here today?"

"I was in the neighborhood and in need of a good meal."
Turning to Mayer, he said. "Let me introduce you to Mayer

Rubin. He's an American. I've been giving him a tour of Jerusalem."

Eying Mayer, Zoltan asked, "Have you eaten Hungarian food before?"

"No, but Professor Taube has raved about your cooking."

"Excellent. Then I'll have to prepare something special."

As the chef headed to the kitchen, a young dark-haired woman appeared and filled their water glasses. As he quenched his thirst, Taube noted how Mayer turned his head and followed her curvaceous body with his eyes until she disappeared into the kitchen. Raising his eyebrows, he teased Mayer. "Attractive girl, isn't she?"

Embarrassed, Mayer lowered his eyes and gulped the water in his glass. Ten minutes into feasting on the paprika-seasoned brisket stew, Mayer placed his fork and knife on his empty plate and gazed at Taube. "Since you mentioned it earlier today, I've been thinking about the Ark of the Covenant."

"And?"

"Where do you think it could be hidden?"

"There's much written about the mysterious disappearance of the Ark before Solomon's Temple was destroyed by the Babylonians. No one knows for sure, but there's a Bible reference to the prophet and high priest, Jeremiah, moving the Ark to a safe place, perhaps to a secret chamber below the Temple Mount."

Mayer's face flushed with excitement. "A secret chamber?"

"Yes, below the Temple Mount are a series of vaulted chambers referred to as Solomon's stables."

"Has anyone ever explored the chambers?"

"There have been many explorations, but the most important were nine French knights known as the Knights Templar. Stationed in Jerusalem after the first crusade, they lived on the Temple Mount in exchange for protecting visiting pilgrims. While there's no evidence of the Templars ever protecting any travelers in the Holy Land, we do know they excavated and explored the tunnels and chambers below the Temple Mount for nine years."

Sitting on the edge of his chair, Mayer raised his hand in a questioning gesture. "Did they find the Ark?"

"We're not sure, but when they departed for France in 1128, the Templars were known to have transported a large cache of gold, jewels, documents, and ancient Judaic manuscripts that had been sealed in earthen jars centuries earlier."

Mayer wanted to know more about the Ark and the Knights Templar, but before he could ask, Taube cut him off. "It's four o'clock. I'd better drive you back to the rabbi's house."

Taube stopped the Land Rover in front of Rabbi Katz's compound. Mayer jumped out, closed the passenger door, and poked his head through the vehicles open window. "Thank you, Professor. You've given me much to think about."

Taube smiled. "I'm glad you enjoyed Jerusalem, but keep in mind there's so much more to learn."

Mayer inhaled, then said, "If you don't mind, I have one last question."

Taube shifted into neutral and gestured to Mayer with his open hand. "Sure, go ahead."

"Do you think a new temple will be built on the Temple Mount?"

Taube's blue eyes seemed to glow. "One day a new temple will rise on the Temple Mount and within its walls the Ark of the Covenant shall again reside. We can talk more it the next time you visit Jerusalem. Shalom."

Mayer's imagination raced as he watched Taube's Land Rover speed away.

# CHAPTER 30

Katherine Eisen was viewing an album of photographs in her daughter's upstairs bedroom when she heard the sound of the garage door opening. *That's strange; it's only a quarter of five. Couldn't be Max, he's rarely home before six-thirty.*

Worried that she may have forgotten to lock the kitchen door leading to the garage, she raced down the staircase. But as she reached the kitchen, the door abruptly sprung open. There in the doorway stood Max. "Kate—you look surprised."

"I am," she said, admonishing him. "You're never home so early."

Max stared at her. "Is something wrong?"

"No," she snapped back. "I'm just a little nervous, that's all. There've been two break-ins in the neighborhood in the last month." A moment later, her mouth curled into a smile. "Sorry. I didn't mean to jump at you. You alright?"

Max smiled, then kissed her. "I've had an awful day, so I decided to leave the office early. Why don't we go out and have a beer and a burger at the Mason Jar."

Katherine pushed her auburn hair back from her face and smiled. "That's a great idea. I don't feel like cooking and I could use a drink."

"What about Morgan?"

"Oh, she's having dinner at her friend's house and will probably sleep over."

Familiar with the menu at the Mason Jar, a local eatery known for its charbroiled burgers and barbecued ribs, they both ordered medium rare burgers and steins of Sam Adam's Ale on draft.

While they waited for their order, Katherine noted the drawn look on her husband's face. "Want to tell me what's bothering you?"

Max sighed. "The information Harry uncovered on Mayer Rubin upsets me. At stake is everything I've worked for in the last five years. If I don't complete the new round of financing, the company could go down the drain." Max paused. "And you know what that means for us."

Katherine reached across the table and pressed Max's hand. "Have you been in touch with Harry?"

"Sure. We talked on the phone last week. He said he'd be on the west coast for several days, but would call sometime this week."

"Don't worry, sweetheart. He'll be in touch." Grasping her beer stein, she flashed a playful smile. "Let's have some fun!"

Max raised his beer stein and forced a smile. "You know Kate, even on the gloomiest of days you have a special knack for lifting my spirits. Here's to you."

When they returned home, Max found a message waiting on his answering machine. McClure had called and left a number at a hotel in San Francisco. Sounding upbeat, he requested Max call him after eight Pacific Time.

"See? I told you so," Kate gloated.

"As usual, you're right."

Smiling flirtatiously, she kissed Max's lips. "I think you could use some TLC. Remember, we have the house to ourselves tonight."

# CHAPTER 31

For Mayer, following a stimulating experience in Jerusalem, the routine of the Bobov Yeshiva study program was a letdown.

Several days later, feeling tired, he headed to his room through the long corridor connecting the main yeshiva building with the student dormitories.

During the day, a row of small rectangular windows on both sides of the wall, spaced two feet below the ten-foot high ceiling, filled the corridors with white light. In the evening, frosted glass sconces mounted on the walls fifteen feet apart illuminated the corridors.

On many occasions, Mayer had stopped to view one or more of the paintings of the famous Tzedek rebbes lining the walls of the corridor, but on this evening he passed them without stopping. His thoughts instead were on Professor

Taube's stimulating narrative of the Temple Mount and the Ark of the Covenant.

Just as he approached the portrait of Rebbe Halberstram, the unexpected pop of a light bulb jarred him. Looking down the length of the corridor in both directions, he confirmed he was alone. *Perhaps it was a sign from God.* Just in case, he recited a special silent prayer for his mentor's good health and long life.

By eleven-thirty, as he readied for bed, Mayer heard an unexpected knock at his door. Pressing his ear to the door, he called out, "Who is it?"

A muffled voice answered, "It's Yossi. I need to talk to you. Open the door."

"Just a minute." Mayer grabbed a robe from his closet and opened the door. To his surprise, in the hallway stood Yossi Abramowitz dressed in a white linen robe, a large prayer shawl draped over his shoulders.

"Come in," Mayer said. But he wondered, *what's this about?*

Yossi quietly closed the door behind him and motioned for Mayer to sit on a chair adjacent to his bed.

"You know, you're not the same young man who came here from America a year ago."

Mayer nodded, but his instincts told him Yossi's late night visit was more than a social call. "Is something wrong?" he asked nervously."

"No," Yossi replied. "I just need to ask you a few questions, and then I'll tell you why I'm here tonight. Is that alright?"

"Yes, of course," Mayer replied without hesitating.

Gazing into Mayer's eyes, Yossi asked, "Do you believe there is but one eternal omnipotent God?"

Again Mayer answered, "Yes, of course."

"And do you believe Israel is the rightful homeland of the Jewish people?"

Though Mayer thought, *these are strange questions*, he replied, "Yes."

Yossi smiled approvingly.

A look of apprehension on his face, Mayer asked, "Is there something else?"

Yossi nodded. "There is."

"Well, what is it?" Mayer pressed, raising his voice.

"I'm here to extend an invitation for you to join a special secret brotherhood."

Not sure he had heard Yossi correctly, in a cautious tone Mayer repeated, "An invitation to join a secret brotherhood?"

"Yes. A brotherhood dedicated to carrying out God's work on behalf of the chosen people."

Though perplexed, Mayer motioned for Yossi to continue.

"Before I can go further, you must give me your word. Under no circumstance will you ever repeat what I'm about to share with you. If you break your promise, your life will be in great danger."

Mayer studied Yossi's face. There was a serious look in his dark eyes. *What could be so important that I could chance losing my life? If I say no, then I'll be ostracized. If I say yes, I may put my life in danger.* His mind churned. Holding his hand to his mouth, he thought. "Okay, Yossi. I'll put my trust in you. I promise to keep this matter a secret."

Yossi placed his hand on Mayer's shoulder and smiled. "I was hoping you'd say yes. Get dressed and follow me."

# CHAPTER 32

Mayer trailed a few steps behind Yossi along the same corridor which he had passed through less than an hour earlier. In front of the floor-length portrait of Rebbe Halberstram, Yossi stopped and scanned the corridor in both directions. Satisfied that they were alone, he reached behind the upper corner of the portrait's ornate frame and released a concealed lever. Cleverly designed, the frame remained stationary while the painting of Rebbe Halberstram silently swung into the wall. Motioning to Mayer, in a hushed voice he said, "Follow me. Be careful."

Inside the darkened tunnel, Yossi activated his flashlight and focused the beam of light on a grey metal box mounted to the wall containing a red and green button. He pressed the red button and waited until the concealed door closed. Then he pressed the green button. Instantaneously, a series of lamps mounted along the walls illuminated the arched narrow tunnel.

Astonished, Mayer asked, "What is this place?"

Yossi replied in a hushed tone, "A short time before Israeli declared her sovereignty in 1948, this tunnel and the chambers ahead were constructed as bomb shelters. All but forgotten, in 1958 an excavation team preparing the ground for construction of the new yeshiva complex buildings unearthed its existence. Fortunately, the tunnel was saved and enhanced."

Continuing another twenty-five feet, they came to a heavy metal door. Yossi inserted a credit card sized object into a narrow horizontal slit on the right side of the door. A moment later, a green diode flashed, and the reinforced metal door slowly opened.

A tall bearded man clad in a white linen robe, with a large prayer shawl over his head, stood in the doorway. "Shalom." Turning to Mayer, the figure brusquely ordered, "Take off all your clothing and put on this tunic."

Uneasy, Mayer looked to Yossi for guidance.

"It's all right," Yossi reassured.

Though nervous, Mayer complied with the order of the solemn-faced man.

Yossi grasped Mayer's arm and led him through another tunnel leading to a large candlelit room dominated by the flickering light of a stately golden menorah.

On a raised marble platform, behind the kingly Boaz and the priestly Jachin pillars, reminiscent of King Solomon's

Temple, stood the high priest. He was wearing a white linen hat with a scarlet stripe and an elegant plaid ceremonial apron (ephod) of fine linen intricately woven with gold, blue, and scarlet thread clasped together at the shoulder by onyx stones set in gold. On his chest hung a breastplate arranged in three rows containing twelve precious stones set in gold. Inscribed on each stone in Hebrew letters was the name of one of the twelve ancient biblical tribes of Israel.

Behind the high priest stood ten men dressed in white linen robes, large prayer shawls covering their heads. Chanting an ancient Davidic psalm, the men rhythmically rocked the upper part of their bodies in unison.

Seemingly charged with mystical power, the energy flowing within the candlelit room was enhanced by an ethereal white light emanating from a rectangular opening high above the pyramid-shaped vaulted ceiling. When the high priest raised his gold scepter, the men behind him stopped chanting and stood motionless. Gazing down from the marble altar, he called out, "We welcome you, Mayer Rubin."

To his amazement, Mayer recognized the voice of the high priest. *It's Rabbi Katz.* He also identified the unmistakable figure of Professor Taube. *What's this all about?*

Following a moment of silence, the high priest continued, "The men gathered here tonight have deemed you worthy of joining our brotherhood. I ask you now—do you accept the trust we place in you to carry out God's mission whenever you're called upon and never to reveal our secrets to anyone, even if your life is at risk?"

Mayer felt as though he were standing at the edge of a high cliff, unsure of his balance. Darting a quick glance at Yossi standing on the marble altar four positions to the left of the high priest, he thought he glimpsed him nodding affirmatively, but couldn't be sure. Once again, he would have to rely on his instincts. Mustering all his courage, he replied, "Yes. I do."

"Then come forward and join us," the high priest commanded.

Mayer walked to the left side of the elevated platform. Met by Professor Taube, he was guided to a position just left of the high priest.

On a signal from the high priest, the white robed men then formed a semi-circle around Mayer. Suddenly, he felt multiple hands grasp his body. A moment later, he was lying flat on his back looking up at a circle of faces that stared at him from above. *My God, I'm in some sort of a grave. Are they going to kill me?*

Following an anxiety-filled period of silence, he again felt multiple hands grasp his body. This time, they carefully lifted and placed him erect on the elevated platform.

The high priest draped a large shawl over Mayer's head and lit a tall white candle. Then, extending his arms above his head in the direction of the ethereal light emanating from high above the altar, his powerful resonant voice reverberating against the vaulted ceiling, he recited a sacred Hebrew prayer.

Turning to Mayer, he raised his scepter. "You've been reborn. We welcome you as a member of the ancient Essene Brotherhood. Now and forever more, as a Son of Light, be faithful to our mission and guard our secrets with your life." Withdrawing a rectangular gold pendant inlaid with three concentric cobalt blue lines from a compartment in the altar, he placed the pendant around Mayer's neck.

The high priest continued. "Never reveal to anyone your membership in the Essene Brotherhood, our mission, or the names of our members. If you break your vow, the penalty will be severe. Wherever you go and whatever you do, always wear the Essene pendant. It will protect you from all harm. May God bless and guide you."

With a sway of his scepter, the high priest concluded the initiation ceremony.

# CHAPTER 33

S till in a state of shock, Mayer joined his new Essene brothers at a special banquet in another cavernous room within the elaborate underground system. As the guest of honor, he sat at the narrow end of a long rectangular wooden table facing the high priest. The high priest recited prayers for the bread they were about to eat and the wine they were about to drink, then called upon each Essene member to introduce themselves.

Shlomo Fried, a retired army lieutenant colonel connected with Mossad, was one of the Essenes who introduced himself to Mayer. He had been the mysterious man driving the jeep on Mayer's first trip to Jerusalem.

When all members had taken their turn, the high priest raised his scepter and offered a special prayer requesting God to bless and guide their holy mission. The banquet was reminiscent of typical fare served during the reign of King

Solomon. Served on white china plates adorned with the three blue concentric lines symbolizing the three walls surrounding Herod's Temple, it consisted of roasted meats, grilled chicken, and braised vegetables.

While they dined, Yossi revealed to Mayer, "Our leader and high priest, Rabbi Katz, is a Golan Kohein. He's a direct descendent of Aaron, the first high priest and elder brother of Moses. A Golan Kohein, the high priest of Solomon's Temple, was the only person, and only on Yom Kippur, permitted to enter the sanctuary of God containing the Ark of the Covenant."

From the day he took an oath to follow the tenets of the Essene Brotherhood, whether he completely understood his oath or not, Mayer had committed himself to the code of the secret Essene Brotherhood for life.

An unusual alliance of Hasidic and non-Hasidic Ultra-Orthodox Jews, the Essenes had adopted the name of a secretive orthodox sect that flourished in Qumran more than two thousand years earlier.

As with their namesake, the Essene Brotherhood committed itself to three fundamental objectives: the rebirth of Israel as a theocratic Jewish State, the return of the Ark of the Covenant to the Jerusalem Temple, and the fulfillment of an ancient Messianic prophecy. Whatever the cost, no matter how long it would take, their mission, they believed, would be guided by their total and unwavering commitment to God.

# CHAPTER 34

Max dialed the number McClure had left on his answering machine. A moment later, a crisp female voice said, "Pan Pacific Hotel. How may I help you?"

"I'd like to speak with Harry McClure."

"One moment please."

McClure responded on the second ring. "Hello?"

"Harry, it's Max."

"I'm glad you got my message. You alright?"

"Yeah, I'm fine. Katherine and I were out to dinner when you called. What's up?"

"I've been thinking about Mayer Rubin's transfer of his stock to yeshivas in Boro Park."

In a mocking tone, Max laughed.

"What's so funny?"

"You mean the stock Mayer said he donated to further God's work."

"That's what I'm referring to."

"What about it?"

"I recall you saying that soon after Mayer's generous donation, the yeshivas contacted Federman and requested removal of legends on their shares."

"That's right. And based on Federman's advice, I had no legal right to withhold signing off on the new stock certificates."

"I think I can fill in the scenario that followed. A short time after the new certificates were issued non-public company information, which I suspect they overheard when they bugged your office, was fed to their boiler-room brokers.

"In turn, the brokers then fed the information to unsuspecting investors eager to get in on a hot stock tip. The increased buying activity resulted in a dramatic upward blip in the price of your stock. Within a few weeks, the stock was up at least fifty percent, in some cases seventy-five percent. The yeshiva then sold its block of shares. Now here's the best part."

"There's more?"

"Yes. I'm sure you've heard the term short-selling?"

"Sure. It's when you borrow and sell stock you don't own with the intention of repurchasing the stock when the price of the stock has fallen."

"That's right. So, soon after the yeshiva sale cleared, Mayer's agents started short selling your company's stock. Rigging the market, they caused the price of your thinly traded stock to fall to a point that covered their short sales at a sizeable profit. Then, once again, their boiler room accomplices stepped in and targeted another group of unsuspecting investors."

"It makes sense, but how did you figure out how their scheme operates?"

McClure chuckled. "I have to confess. I had some assistance from my old friend, Stan Jacob. He mentioned he would call you."

"He did, Harry, We had a lengthy telephone discussion a few days ago. He asked a lot of probing questions about Mark Federman."

"That's not surprising. My instincts tell me Mark Federman is somehow involved in Mayer Rubin's scheme. Federman maintains a low profile, but we're following his paper trail."

Holding the phone receiver to his ear, Max swiveled his chair around and looked at a framed picture of himself, Mayer Rubin, and Mark Federman taken at NovoMed's first public shareholder meeting. "Imagine, six months ago we were paying Federman's bloated legal bills." Max groaned. "When will you be back in New York?"

"I'm leaving San Francisco tomorrow evening on the red eye. Can you meet me at my office on Thursday morning, say eleven?"

"Sure. That's fine."

"I've asked Stan Jacob to join us. By then we'll also have a follow-up report from Bob Jones."

# CHAPTER 35

In the weeks following his initiation as an Essene Brotherhood member, Mayer continued with his daily yeshiva study program. On many evenings, however, he would break away and join his fellow Essene brothers.

Within the Essene enclave, Yossi introduced Mayer to the ancient Essene ritualistic purification bath.

"Many biblical scholars," Yossi said, "believe that John the Baptist, after visiting Qumran, adopted the concept of the Essene ritualistic baths as a form of spiritual resurrection."

Mayer sneered. "So that's where the Catholic Church got the idea of baptism from."

He was developing a close relationship with Professor Taube. During one of their many discussions, Taube related the story of an Israeli archeological team who, during an exploration of the caves of Qumran, discovered several scrolls wrapped in papyrus.

"Unlike any of the previously discovered scrolls," Taube said, "these were marked with three concentric blue lines. After considerable research, my team realized the three blue lines represent the Jerusalem Temple built during the reign of King Herod the Great. The scrolls also shed new light on the mysterious power of the Ark of the Covenant and where it may have been secretly hidden for safekeeping.

"You may recall, when you first visited Jerusalem, I told you the Knights Templar had come to the Holy Land in 1118 under the guise of protecting travelers who visited the Holy land. Their true mission, however, was to recover secret ancient Judaic documents and a large cache of gold and silver hidden under the Temple Mount by temple priests and the Essenes before the temple was destroyed by the Romans."

Mayer's eyes widened with excitement.

Taube went on. "Using the Al Aqsa Mosque as their headquarters in Jerusalem, the Templars dug into the bedrock and discovered many hidden chambers. In one of the chambers they uncovered scrolls documenting how the Prophet Jeremiah, fearing the imminent destruction of Solomon's Temple by the Babylonians, removed the Ark and many of the holy treasures from the Temple and hid them in a cave at the base of Mt. Sinai."

"You mean the mountain where Moses received the Ten Commandments from God?"

Taube nodded.

"Do you know where the cave is located?"

"I have some ideas, but I don't think the Ark is there anymore."

Mayer raised his eyebrow. "I don't understand. Where is it?"

"Near the end of the Christian occupation of Palestine in 1182, a young English Templar knight, Ralph de Sudeley, joined the Templars in Jerusalem. A short time later, he was assigned command of a small garrison south of Jerusalem, near the ancient city of Petra. I believe he may have found the Ark and a considerable quantity of jewels and gold objects hidden by Jeremiah in a cave like building called the Treasury.

"But two years later, the Muslims recaptured Jerusalem and forced the Crusaders to abandon their castles in the Edom Valley."

"Do you know where the Ark is now?"

A faint knowing expression on his face, Taube replied, "We have some clues. It will take time and money to recover the Ark, but I'm confident that it will be found and returned to its rightful place on the Temple Mount."

As Mayer relaxed on an El Al flight bound for New York, he noted the seatbelt light was turned off. A few minutes later, a flight attendant began serving the first of several kosher meals and beverages.

Soon after the cabin crew collected the empty food trays, with the exception of the constant drone of the aircraft engines, the cabin went quiet. While most passengers slept, Mayer's eyes scanned the aisle, then behind his seat. Satisfied that he was not being observed, he lowered his window shade and placed his travel bag on the empty middle seat. Holding a black leather-bound Hebrew Bible in his hand, he thought of his fourteen-month stay in Israel. Arriving a day before the onset of the Six-Day War, he was for the first time in his life unexpectedly thrust into a life-threatening situation. Guided by dedicated teachers, he had mastered Yiddish, learned to read and write in Hebrew, studied the Torah and Jewish law

(Halakhah), and had acquired an understanding of the Talmud and the mystical teachings of the Kabbalah.

The long black coat, the black hat, the full beard, peyos, and the daily ritual praying he fully accepted as part of his chosen Hasidic lifestyle, but he was still acclimating to another dimension of his new life—his membership in the secret Essene Brotherhood.

As he clutched the rectangular gold pendant, inscribed with the three concentric blue lines suspended from a thin gold chain he wore around his neck, Mayer thought of Yossi Abramowitz's words. *Like the ancient Essenes who, in their commitment to God, endured the harsh environment of the Qumran desert, so we must be patient and await God's calling. When the time is right, we shall be ready.*

Late in the evening, in the privacy of his yeshiva room, Mayer had practiced opening the specially designed Hebrew Bible to the first page of Deuteronomy. Pressing the front and back covers together, he exposed a concealed compartment containing a page of instructions on how to write and decipher the code.

He unfolded a sheet of paper inserted into the first page of Exodus and deciphered the note Yossi had given to him as they drove to the airport. *Drgs Tlw'h yovhhrmt, Gsv Vhhvmv Yilgsvisllw droo lmv wzb ivyfrow gsv Gvnkov zmw ivgfim Tlw'h hzmxgfzib, Gsv Zip lu Gsv Xlevmzmg, gl rgh irtsgufo slnv lm gsv Gvnkov Nlfmg.*

Proud of himself, he folded and placed the encoded page in his shirt pocket, then returned the Bible to his travel bag. Positioning a pillow behind his head, he switched off the overhead reading light and drifted off to sleep.

# CHAPTER 37

Rebbe Halberstram dispatched a young member of his congregation to meet Mayer at Kennedy Airport. Taller and several years older than Mayer, Hershel Weinberg's wavy reddish brown peyos, draping down both sides of his face, flowed from a shaven head under a large black hat. Unlike Mayer, he was born and raised in the Bobov Hasidic community in Boro Park.

While he firmly gripped the steering wheel of the 1966 Oldsmobile Vista-Cruiser station wagon, Weinberg viewed the image of Mayer in the rear view mirror. "I understand you were in Israel during the Six-Day War?"

A smug grin on his face, Mayer replied, "Yes, I was in the midst of the shooting."

Weinberg adjusted the rear view mirror and continued questioning Mayer. "Were you ever in any danger?"

Mayer nodded. He enjoyed Hershel Weinberg's questions; they made him feel important. "Oh, yes, many times. The Arabs were everywhere—shooting and killing innocent Jewish women and children."

"Were you scared?"

"Sure, but I knew God would protect me."

"And, did you get to pray at the Wall?"

"Mayer smiled proudly. "Yes. In fact, after the Israeli Army recaptured Jerusalem, I was among the first group of Jews allowed to pray at the Wall. I can tell you, as I prayed at the Wall, I truly sensed God's presence."

Weinberg parked the station wagon in front of the rebbe's house, then turned to Mayer. "Perhaps one day, I too will have the opportunity to pray at the Wall."

"Perhaps you will. It's all up to God."

Suitcase in hand, Mayer knocked on the rebbe's door and waited. He was about to knock again when the door opened and an elderly woman, a scarf wrapped over her head, greeted him. "Please come in, Mr. Rubin. The rebbe is waiting for you in his study."

Before entering the rebbe's house, Mayer touched the mezuzah mounted to the right side of the doorframe with his outstretched fingers, then quickly pressed them to his lips. Leaving his suitcase in the hallway, he proceeded to the rebbe's study. In a corner of the dimly lit room, an elderly grey-bearded man hunched over a large oak desk sat reading an old prayer book.

The rebbe lifted his eyes and beckoned Mayer to join him. As Mayer approached, he rose from his desk, extended his hand, and embraced him. Returning to his desk, he motioned for Mayer to sit in a chair in front of his desk. Gazing fondly at Mayer, he said in Yiddish, "I'm happy to see you again. We're blessed with your safe return. So tell me, did your trip to Israel go well?"

Mayer, his skin tingling, smiled. "Wonderful! More than I could have ever have imagined. You were right, of course, in suggesting I study in Israel. I'm looking forward to going back before too long."

"I'm gratified to hear that your trip was rewarding."

Mayer was not sure what the rebbe meant. *Did he know of my membership in the secret Essene Brotherhood?* He dared not ask.

"I've received an excellent report from your yeshiva teachers," the rebbe said in a fatherly voice.

Elated, Mayer thanked him for his generosity and wisdom.

The rebbe leaned back and clasped his hands together. "Do you remember the conversation we had before you left for Israel?"

Mayer nodded. "Yes."

"Are you prepared to fully accept our way of life and devotion to God?"

Mayer inhaled. He could feel his heart beating rapidly. "Yes, I'm ready and committed."

"Then I'm pleased to welcome you as a member of our congregation. You'll stay in my home for a few days, and then you'll go to live with another member of our congregation, David Ostroff. He is a respected diamond merchant. If you like, he can arrange for you to apprentice in the diamond business."

Mayer smiled. "I'd like to learn the diamond business."

"Good. Go and freshen up, and then join us for dinner at six-thirty. If you go down the hall, you'll find my wife in the kitchen. She'll show you to your room. I'll see you at dinner."

*As a protégé of the rebbe*, Mayer thought, *I'll be readily acceptable to the Hasidim who dominate New York's 47th Street diamond market.*

# CHAPTER 38

Ten years earlier, a young Hasidic student on his first trip to Israel recited a solemn vow to uphold the tenets of a secret Judaic society, the Essene Brotherhood. Now married, the father of five children and fully assimilated into the Boro Park Hasidic community, on the surface he appeared content. Secretly, however, he was frustrated by the daily routine of the job he held in New York's Forty-Seventh Street Diamond Exchange.

A chance meeting with a stockbroker friend provided the opportunity Mayer sought. Resourceful, he soon arranged to meet a group of young stockbrokers employed at Datek Securities, a highflying Brooklyn-based brokerage firm.

The ambitious stockbrokers taught Mayer the fundamentals of stock trading in return for Mayer referring customers to them. Eager to begin stock trading, his annual Passover family trip to Israel provided an ideal opportunity to discuss his business plans with the Essene leadership.

Welcomed by fellow Essene brothers, Mayer once again joined in their secret gatherings and assisted in the initiation of several new members. When he entered the Essene compound through the same hidden door he had passed through as a young initiate 10 years earlier, he noted the large quantity of arms, munitions, and food supplies stockpiled in wooden cases along the corridors. "What's going on?" he asked Yossi.

"To avoid detection, we're gradually building up an inventory of weapons and supplies. When the time is right, we'll need the weapons and much more."

Sensing a hand on his shoulder, Mayer turned and gazed up into Professor Taube's penetrating blue eyes. Tanned and looking fit, he welcomed Mayer, then guided him to a windowless office crammed with archeological maps. After they chatted for several minutes, Mayer asked, "How is your search for the Ark of the Covenant going?"

Taube smiled. "I'm glad you haven't forgotten our discussion."

"No, I haven't. Since the first time you mentioned the Ark, it has intrigued me."

"Well, the answer is a qualified yes. We think we know where the Ark is, but it will take considerable effort and ingenuity to recover."

"Where do you think it is?"

Taube leaned back in his chair and gazed at Mayer. "This may surprise you, but I think it's in Scotland."

"Scotland?"

Taube nodded. "Yes. Hidden within the last home and sanctuary of the Knights Templar—Rosslyn Chapel."

His eyes filled with excitement, Mayer raised his index finger. "Oh yes, now I remember. The first time I visited Jerusalem, you mentioned the Knights Templar, but you didn't say where you thought the Ark was hidden. Can it be recovered?"

"I think so. With God's help, we intend to recover The Ark and return it to its rightful place on the Temple Mount."

Before returning to New York, Mayer requested a private meeting with the high priest, Rabbi Katz, and Yossi Abramowitz.

When he entered the meeting room, he was surprised to see, in addition to Rabbi Katz and Yossi, two other men. He recognized Shlomo Fried, but the other man he had not met before.

Rabbi Katz motioned for Mayer to sit, then he introduced Eli Pinski. "I've asked Eli to join us today. He's a fellow Essene and a Vice President of Bank Leumi. His specialty is the U.S. financial markets."

Mayor eyed the clean-shaven, thin man dressed in an open collar white shirt sitting across from him and forced a smile. Then he turned his head and gazed at the rabbi.

"We'd like to hear your thoughts on the Wall Street project you've expressed interest in pursuing," the rabbi said.

Mayer nodded and launched into a 30-minute oral presentation. When he finished, he fielded several questions, then the room went quiet.

With the tips of his fingers touching, the rabbi surveyed the faces of the other three Essene members, then his eyes locked on Mayer.

"We think investing in early stage companies in the U.S. may prove beneficial to the realization of our ultimate objectives. When you return to New York, I want you to contact one of our brothers, Mark Federman. He's a securities attorney and an expert in complex financial transactions. I'm sure he can help you. Yossi will give you the details on how to contact him. As always, exercise care and be guided by the power of God."

# CHAPTER 39

Heartened by the support he'd received from the Essene leadership during his Passover visit to Israel, Mayer returned to New York and plunged into expanding his sphere of Wall Street contacts.

Knowing he needed a registered stockbroker as an accomplice, he set his sights on Barr Securities. The firm, managed by a group of shrewd investment bankers, had made a name for itself by specializing in underwriting early stage companies, many of which had not yet reached profitability.

Through a friend in the diamond trade, he arranged to meet a young Hasidic stockbroker who recently joined the firm. Mordacai Shulman had previously worked at several second tier brokerage firms.

Two years younger than Mayer and recently married, Shulman was a member of the Lubavitch Hasidic sect. He and Mayer became fast friends, or so Shulman believed. In truth,

Mayer, aside from members of the clandestine Essene Brotherhood, had few real friends, only people he exploited for his own gain.

During his years at the 47th Street Diamond Exchange, Mayer had befriended many wealthy Hasidim who, though interested in lucrative investments, were reluctant to entrust their money to anyone outside of their own orthodox community. As he prepared to launch his new venture, Mayer discovered that Shulman, at each new public underwriting, was allocated a block of stock that often doubled or even tripled on the opening day. *What a perfect opportunity.*

On a sunny spring afternoon after the market closed, as they walked past Trinity Church in lower Manhattan, Mayer turned to Shulman. "You know I have many contacts in the Diamond Exchange who are seeking attractive investments. Perhaps we can work together." The following day Shulman offered to compensate Mayer for business he referred.

Mayer thanked Shulman for his generosity and suggested an even bolder arrangement. "You and I are like brothers. Why not be partners? Since our parents lost so much in the Holocaust, knowing their sons are financially independent would bring them much joy."

Shulman wholeheartedly endorsed Mayer's plan several days later. Mayer would deliver the business, Shulman would execute the trades and they would split the commissions.

Mayer knew the scheme under NASD regulations was illegal, so he reassured Shulman, "Don't worry. Only you and I will know."

Mayer had primed the right accomplice, the person he needed for entry into the brokerage community and access to the new issues market.

With steady income from new accounts opened in Shulman's name, Mayer began spending more time at Barr Securities and less time in the 47th Street Diamond Exchange. As business grew, they began to visit brokerage firms Mayer termed "potential business friends." Small, often marginally capitalized, they welcomed new customers.

Mayer also opened many doors with a clever pitch. "We represent a lot of private money in the Hasidic community and are looking for investment opportunities."

Word soon filtered back to another aspiring Wall Street manipulator. Tony Ribaldi grew up in a middle-class Italian family on Staten Island. A longtime friend recalled of him, "Tony was always a hustler."

A short time after he graduated from high school, Ribaldi enlisted in the Army. Two months later, he was sent to Vietnam. Upon discharge from the Army, he enrolled in an accounting program at Pace College. Taking advantage of the GI bill, he attended night school while working as an insurance agent during the day. Armed with an accounting degree, he talked himself into a stockbroker-training program at Walston & Company and stayed for a little over two years. A succession of similar positions followed with other well-known brokerage firms, but always looking for a better deal, he never fit in.

Soon after Ribaldi married a woman who worked in his office, he decided the time was right to launch his own brokerage firm.

With her family's financial backing, he chose the established sounding name of Pierpont Securities for his new firm.

In the early 80's, with the country in the midst of a frenzied interest in the stock market, he quickly latched on to several early stage medical technology companies. All of the companies had a common denominator: A good story to tell and a need for cash. Mayer had found another important ally.

Pierpont Securities second IPO, Argon Medical, turned into an instant success. To bolster the underwriting, several Boro Park yeshivas controlled by Mayer received a commitment for the purchase of a large block of Argon shares at $2.50. The stock opened at $4 and within three weeks, shot up to $15. By the end of the month, the stock had risen to $20, but by then all of the investors Mayer controlled had sold their holdings at $19 to $20 per share. Overnight the stock retreated to its initial opening price of $4. Tony Ribaldi had demonstrated to Mayer and Shulman how their alliance could be mutually beneficial.

A short time later, to celebrate his success, Mayer purchased a large sable hat for $3,000. Called a Stremmel, he proudly wore it on the Sabbath and holidays. A status symbol in the Boro Park Hassidic community, he boasted to Shulman, "I think it's only fitting for a man of my stature to own the finest hat."

Shulman agreed.

Mayer now began to talk of doing bigger deals. He was confident the support of the Essene Brotherhood would play an important role in helping to make his dream a reality.

# CHAPTER 40

On his way to McClure's New York office, with traffic unusually light, Max zipped across the George Washington Bridge in his Saab convertible. As he exited onto the southbound lane of the Henry Hudson Parkway, he caught view of the fully rigged Chilean training ship, the Esmeralda. Shadowed by a half a dozen smaller sailing ships, she was sailing south on a course that would take her under the Verrazano Bridge and out to the open sea.

For a brief moment, just before exiting on 79th Street, Max fantasized that he was the captain of a sleek sailing craft as its racing spinnaker caught the wind.

*Enough of that*, he thought. *I've got to channel my resources into saving my company.* Cutting across Central Park at 78th Street, he drove south on Park Avenue and found a garage on East 56th Street.

As the elevator in McClure's brownstone opened on the second floor, Velma greeted him.

"I'm a little early. Traffic was lighter than usual."

"No problem," she said, smiling. "Follow me." Stopping in front of the conference room door, she motioned with her hand. "Go right in."

# CHAPTER 41

As Max entered the conference room, McClure rose and gestured to the figure sitting across from him. "I think you already met Stan Jacob, at least on the phone."

"We have," Max said, extending his hand across the conference table.

Jacob rose and shook Max's hand. "I've been looking forward to our meeting."

Broad shouldered, with angular features and a full head of white hair, the scholarly looking Stanley Jacob preferred dark blue pin-striped vested suits. A Yale graduate and Fulbright Scholar, his background and expertise ranked him as one of most sought after SEC attorneys in the country. Before he joined the prestigious law firm of Friedman, Moskowitz, Reilly, and Pope as senior partner in charge of corporate law and SEC compliance, Jacob had directed the enforcement division of the SEC in Washington, DC. A seasoned corporate law attorney, he was also an expert in the intricacies of the financial markets.

"Stan, perhaps you can take it from here."

Jacob nodded. "Sure, Harry." Opening a large brown accordion folder, he fixed his eyes on Max. "Reviewing all of your SEC filings, beginning with your first private placement, I noted that all of the documents were, from a legal perspective, expertly prepared and adhere to SEC standards and regulations.

"Nevertheless, after an initial comparison of the NovoMed documents with the documents on the 10 other companies Mayer Rubin had interest in and Mark Federman served as counsel, the similarity of the documents raised my curiosity."

Darting a glance at McClure, Jacob continued, "I couldn't find anything materially wrong, so I asked an associate to prepare an in-depth graphic analysis of your company compared to the other 10 companies. Reading the article Harry had sent me heightened my suspicions."

"Which article?" Max asked.

"I'm referring to Mayer Rubin's indictment by a federal grand jury that appeared in the *Wall Street Journal.*"

Max's jaw tightened. "I remember that infamous article all too well."

Jacob noted Max's reaction, then continued. "The assertions in the article reinforced my misgivings, so I pulled up the full federal indictment. Mayer Rubin, the indictment alleges, lent yeshivas in Boro Park sizeable sums of money which the yeshivas then illegally invested on his behalf."

Folding his hands together, Max sighed.

Jacob reached into his briefcase, pulled out a folder containing several spreadsheets, and passed a copy to Max, then to McClure. "These two charts will be helpful to our discussion. Please take a moment to review them."

Along the side of the spreadsheets, running vertically down the page, with the exception of NovoMed Corporation appearing at the top of the list, were 10 companies listed alphabetically. At the top of the chart running horizontally were ten headings, beginning with date of incorporation, state of incorporation, date of first private placement, public underwriting, price of shares immediately following underwriting, current price, name of CEO at time of incorporation, current CEO, number of shares outstanding, and corporate counsel. The second chart, in graphic form, represented each company's share price history, starting with the company's initial public offering and ending with its most recent SEC filing.

When he finished examining the chart, Max glanced at McClure and shook his head. "It's hard to believe." Eyeing the second chart, Max said, "If I read this chart correctly, it demonstrates a clear pattern of our stock, as well as the stock of the other companies, rising and falling at predictable times."

A subtle smile on his face, Jacob replied, "Yes, you read the chart correctly. It ties in with the information on the first chart and demonstrates how their scheme operates. All of the companies, after completing initial private placements, were undercapitalized. Each required significantly greater capitalization to complete development of their products, and each, though not profitable, was publicly traded within 18 to 30 months following incorporation.

"Now, Max," Jacob said, referring to a note he had written to himself in the margin of the report, "here's where I need a bit of clarification. What prompted you to consider a public offering when your company was still in the development stage?"

Max glanced at McClure, then focused on Jacob. "Eighteen months after NovoMed completed its initial private placement, product development was on target, but like so many startup companies we needed additional capital to realize our marketing objectives. I had prepared an updated business plan detailing how the infusion of new capital would be used to begin marketing of our first vital signs monitoring system. The goal was to raise $8 million in a private placement."

"What happened with the private placement?"

"At a board meeting, Mayer Rubin volunteered his services to secure funding. Three months later, however, he had arranged only one unsuccessful meeting with a potential funding source. Concerned, I invited him to meet at my office."

Jacob listened and jotted down notes.

"When Mayer arrived an hour late, he told me that due to unforeseen difficulties, the private placement would probably require additional time to complete. Alarmed, I pressed him for a definitive timetable. Waving his hand in the air, he said it would depend on market conditions, perhaps three to six months.

"My patience already strained, I lashed out at him. Lowering his eyes, Mayer stroked his beard and appeared to be meditating. A minute or so later, as though a bolt of lightning had struck him, he regained his composure. Gazing up at the ceiling, he gestured with both hands and proclaimed, 'I have, thanks to God, an idea.' "

Jacob rose, removed his suit jacket, and draped it over the chair next to him. A compelling smile on his face, he fixed his gaze on Max. "If you don't mind, I'd like to take a guess at what occurred next?"

"Sure, go ahead."

"Mr. Rubin's exciting proposal was something on this order. This might be an opportune time to consider an IPO. Moreover, he happened to know of a brokerage firm who, more than likely, would be interested in doing the deal."

Max pursed his lips, then said, "That's close. Though I was skeptical, he and Mark Federman convinced the board it was prudent to pursue an IPO. Out of the proceeds, we repaid the bridge loan of $400,000."

Recalling a statement he had read in the NovoMed prospectus, McClure raised his pencil in the air. "Max, wasn't it

Mayer Rubin who arranged for the bridge loan from a company listed in your prospectus as Hertzog-Lubin Pension Trust?"

"Yes, that's the company."

"Well, we checked out Hertzog-Lubin Pension Trust. It turns out it's another fake company Mayer controls."

Max shook his head. "You know," he said disdainfully, "we didn't need the bridge loan. We had sufficient funds in reserve to tide us over, but Mayer insisted the loan would ensure the success of the underwriting. We paid exorbitant interest on the loan and at the same time gave away a large block of warrants as an added incentive."

Max paused and poured a glass of water. Quenching his thirst, he set the glass down and looked at Jacob. "Sorry, I guess I'm upset . . . I should have known better. What do you suggest, counselor?"

Jacob returned to the conference table. Peering over his reading glasses, he looked at Max. "Don't blame yourself. You had no way to know Mayer Rubin's well-oiled machine had targeted your company. In my opinion, however, he couldn't have pulled off a scheme of this magnitude without the help and expertise of an attorney like Mark Federman."

Max looked at McClure, then focused on Jacob.

"From the data we've gathered, there's considerable evidence to suggest Mayer Rubin and his fellow conspirators have manipulated and illegally profited from the trading of your company's stock and the stock of the other ten compa-

nies Harry identified. In addition, they have probably defrauded many other companies and a large number of individual
investors. Their elaborate scheme has demonstrated a flagrant
disregard of state and federal securities laws."

"What's the bottom line?" McClure asked.

"In my opinion, Mayer Rubin and his fellow conspirators
could be charged with multiple counts of stock manipulation,
tax evasion, and racketeering. Conviction on any of these
charges could result in long prison terms."

Jacob turned to Max. "With your permission, I'd like to
initiate a simultaneous dialogue with my contacts at the Justice
Department and the SEC Enforcement Division in Washington."

"That's fine with me," Max replied without hesitating.
"Just let me know how I can be of help."

Jacob nodded. "Gentlemen, I think we've done all we can
do today." As Jacob readied to leave, Max extended his hand
and thanked him.

McClure positioned himself at the conference room
doorway. As Jacob approached, he said, "I'll walk with you to
the elevator."

As they stood in front of the elevator, McClure turned to
Jacob. "Max is an old friend of mine. I'd like to help him out
of this mess."

"I understand, Harry. You know I despise lawyers who
tarnish our profession. One question . . . Is Max telling the
truth?"

McClure eyed Jacob for a long moment, then he smiled. "Absolutely."

A pleased expression on his face, Jacob gripped McClure's hand. "That's good enough for me. I'll be in touch."

When McClure returned to the conference room, he found Max standing in front of one of the large floor to ceiling windows facing the courtyard. His eyes were following Aristotle busily running through and over a series of brightly colored obstacles in a corner of the enclosed courtyard. McClure placed his arm over Max's shoulder. "How's it going?"

An amused expression on his face, Max replied, "I'm okay. I've enjoyed watching your dog play."

McClure smiled. "It's hard for Aristotle to get the exercise he needs in the city, so Bernadette set up the track for him. He loves it."

Stepping back from the window, Max looked at McClure. "I've been thinking about Stan Jacob's incisive comments."

"Yes, Stan is quite an attorney. I don't know if I mentioned it earlier, but before joining the SEC, as a lawyer for the U.S. District Court for the Southern District of New York, he successfully prosecuted a number of well-known Wall Street figures. That's why I asked him to review your SEC filings."

"I'm glad you did. His analysis uncovered a scheme I'd never have spotted."

McClure noted the time on the wall clock. "Bob Jones is scheduled to join us for an update at three-fifteen. When I spoke with him this morning, he said he had new information to share."

# CHAPTER 42

J ones slipped into a black leather chair and removed a manila folder from his attaché case. Setting the folder on the conference table, he recounted how his team had identified the basement of a private residence in Teaneck, NJ as the site of the monitoring station collecting voice transmissions from Max's offices.

"From ten o'clock in the morning until four-thirty in the afternoon, Monday through Thursday, a steady stream of Hasidic men arrived, then silently departed carrying black travel bags. Every two weeks a panel truck backed up to a garage connected to the house. After the men inside the house unloaded the contents, the truck drove off.

"Initially, we had no idea what they were transporting. Only after listening to the translations of their taped discussions did we realize what they were up to."

Max interrupted. "The woman you mentioned several weeks ago, the Holocaust survivor—"

Jones nodded. "Until she translated the tapes, we didn't know what the truck contained or what the men leaving the house were carrying."

"What did the truck contain?" Max asked impatiently.

Jones's smiled. "That's the big surprise. The truck contained stacks of U.S. currency in large denominations."

His eyes locked on Jones, Max blurted, "Cash?"

"Yes. We believe Mayer Rubin is operating an international money laundering operation out of the house in Teaneck."

"You're joking?" a stunned Max shot back.

"No I'm not joking," Jones reiterated. "And, I think we know how the scheme operates. Much of the money generated by the sale of securities held in the name of yeshivas in league with Rubin is deposited into special bank accounts. A week or so later, a portion of the deposit is wire transferred to another yeshiva bank account in Israel. The remainder of the deposit is then withdrawn in cash and unceremoniously delivered to the house in Teaneck for safekeeping."

Shifting his gaze to McClure, Jones continued, "Remember the men leaving with heavy black bags?"

McClure nodded.

"Well, we believe these men were preparing to leave the country on an expense-paid holiday. Some would travel to Toronto by car while the others would fly to Israel. New recruits transport less than $10,000, which under U.S. regulations they are not required to declare. After several successful trips to Israel, Mayer Rubin would then entrust the courier with considerably larger amounts, often in excess of $100,000. The men going to Toronto concealed $100,000, or more, in the trunks of their cars while those flying to Israel wrapped the money in newspapers concealed in their carry-on luggage. Most of the money eventually ends up in Israel."

McClure chimed in. "How long do you think they've been in business?"

"Although our surveillance only started a short time ago, I'd bet this operation has been around for a long time and has laundered staggering sums of money."

McClure shook his head. "Anything else you've uncovered?"

"Yes," Jones replied, darting a glance at Max. "There's one other important piece of information. Mayer Rubin, who has a habit of bragging, often talks with Mark Federman on the phone. On three separate occasions, Federman warned Mayer to be especially careful as 'The Event' is approaching."

"The Event," McClure repeated, drumming his fingers on the conference table.

Jones nodded emphatically. "Yes. Federman used that term. I don't know what to make of it, but I'm confident they're planning something big—soon."

McClure reflected. *Could this be the link to the murder of Uzi Kopelman?* Turning to Max, he said, "After our meeting with Stan Jacob, I thought we understood Mayer Rubin's operation. Obviously, we were wrong. I sense there is another dimension to his scheme. It's late now, but in the morning I'm going to call an old friend in Israel. He's a high ranking Israeli intelligence officer who I think he can help us sort out what their reference to 'The Event' might mean."

McClure had set his radio alarm clock to 4 a.m., but he was awake and sitting on the edge of his bed before the alarm sounded. Careful not to disturb his wife, he silenced the alarm, put on a robe, and tiptoed down the hall to his office.

He dialed an unlisted number in the Jerusalem office of Ariel Davidov and waited. On the second ring, a female voice answered, "Shalom."

"Shalom. This is Harry McClure."

"Oh, hello, Mr. McClure. Isn't it a bit early for you?"

"It is, but I thought I'd catch Ari if I called early."

"I am afraid he isn't here right now, but I can have him call you when he returns."

"What time do you expect him?"

"I think around five. That should be ten your time. Is that alright?"

"Yes. I should be in my office. Thanks."

Her voice changed to a soft tone. "Will we be seeing you in Israel before too long?"

McClure chuckled. "Perhaps."

"That would be nice. Shalom."


Later in the day, McClure reached for the telephone on his desk and pressed the illuminated second line button. "Good evening, Ari."

"Shalom, Harry. Naomi said you tried to reach me."

"Yes. It's in regard to M. Rubin. We uncovered information I think will interest you."

"Excellent. Go ahead."

"During our search of an M. Rubin who might be living in the U.S., we found a Mayer Rubin who's been a director of a startup medical technology company. As it turns out, the company president is an old friend, so I contacted him."

Davidov's voice tightened. "Harry, I trust he's unaware of your assignment for us?"

Annoyed, McClure shot back, "And I thought you knew me better."

For a moment, Davidov was silent. "Sorry. So, what do we have on Mr. Rubin?"

"For starters, Mayer Rubin orchestrated an elaborate scheme that systematically defrauded NovoMed shareholders, as well as many other NASDAQ listed companies."

Fatigued and unsure of the direction McClure was heading, Davidov asked, "How does a scheme to defraud American shareholders pertain to the murder of Uzi Kopelman?"

"I'm not yet sure, but Mayer's group is also laundering large sums of money which ultimately end up in Israeli bank accounts."

Marked by a sudden change in his tone, Davidov began to question McClure. "How many Israeli banks are involved? Do you have any names, and . . ."

McClure went on. "The ringleader, Mayer Rubin, is a Hasidic Jew living in Boro Park, Brooklyn. On several occasions, we recorded him boasting how he moved large sums of money undetected to banks in Israel."

His interest heightened, Davidov pressed for more information. "How has he moved the money?"

"It's a combination of wire transfers and couriers,"

"Do you have the names of the couriers and the banks involved?"

"We do."

"When can you get me the list?"

"I'll fax it over to you today."

"Good. I'll alert Naomi. Anything else I should know?"

"Yes. There's something which came up, we don't quite understand."

"What's that?"

"Mayer Rubin's attorney, a Mark Federman, has on three separate phone calls warned Rubin to be especially careful as 'The Event' is approaching."

"Did you say, 'The Event'?"

"Yes. That's what I said."

For a moment, there was an eerie silence on the line. "Ari, are you still with me?"

"Yes, I've been pondering what the phrase 'The Event' may mean. You know, we've had a number of incidences of money transfers to radicals like Rabbi Meir Kahane, the Israeli politician assassinated in New York last year, so I'm going to launch an immediate investigation. Perhaps, it will turn out to be a false alarm. I hope so, but we can't afford not to be prudent. Along with the list, please send me all you have on Mayer Rubin." Davidov paused. "And thanks, Harry. Shalom."

# CHAPTER 44

The 1991 Passover holiday trip to Israel had special meaning for Mayer Rubin. In a moment of introspection he recalled how his first visit to Israel, 24 years earlier, had affected the course of his life.

Now, as the expensive Shtreimel fur hat and long black shiny patterned Bekishe coat he wore on the Sabbath symbolized, Mayer was a recognized and respected member of the Boro Park Hasidic community. He was the single signature to a seven-figure bank account, the father of six sons and two daughters, and lived in a spacious house in the best section of Boro Park. But unbeknownst to his family and the Hasidic community, he maintained a secret membership in a powerful clandestine society preparing to fulfill an ancient biblical Messianic prophecy.

Recognizing the important financial contributions Mayer had made to fulfill the mission of the Essene Brotherhood,

Rabbi Katz invited him to celebrate Passover—the holiday commemorating the Israelite's Exodus from ancient Egypt—at his home in Jerusalem. There he joined his fellow Essene Brothers and their families in the first night Passover Seder.

Before the Seder ceremony began, Mayer met privately with Rabbi Katz. "Your financial activities in the U.S. have greatly benefited our efforts to acquire the weapons and equipment needed to launch 'The Event' this summer. When Israel is reborn, the world will learn of the Essene Brotherhood."

Mayer's face tingled with elation as he listened to the high priest praise his work.

"As your fellow Essene Brothers hold you in high esteem, I hope one day, before long, you and your family will make Israel your home."

Mayer beamed. With God's help, I've already placed a deposit on a house in Jerusalem."

The rabbi gave an approving nod, then grasped Mayer's arm and guided him through a foyer leading into a large open room specially prepared for the Seder. To honor his service to the Essene Brotherhood, Mayer was assigned the seat to the right of Rabbi Katz at the head of the table. Many familiar faces, including Mayer's sponsor and close friend Yossi Abramowitz, Professor Avraham Taube, Rabbi Nachman and the mysterious Colonel Shlomo Fried, welcomed him.

On the second night of Passover, Mayer was a guest at the home of Professor Taube. He and his wife lived in a spacious townhouse north of Tel Aviv. After the Seder ceremony had ended and other family members had retired for the night, Taube invited Mayer to join him on his balcony overlooking the Mediterranean Sea.

Sitting on padded wicker chairs, from their vantage point high above the water, they could see in the distance a myriad of tiny twinkling lights radiating from ships anchored in the harbor below.

Taube opened a bottle of kosher for Passover white wine, half-filled two glasses, and offered a toast. "To the success of 'The Event.' L'Chayim."

Mayer smiled through his thick beard and returned the toast. "L'Chayim. May God Bless our mission, and to your living 120 years."

Taube set his wine glass down and searched Mayer's face. "How is your health?"

Surprised by Taube's question, Mayer winced. "I'm fine. About a year ago, I had a mild heart attack, but there's nothing to worry about." The discussion of his own health caused Mayer to feel uneasy, so cleverly he changed the subject.

"You know, I've been fascinated by the Ark of the Covenant ever since you told me it may have been found by the Templar Knights during the Crusades."

A pleased glint in his eyes, Taube placed his arm over Mayer's shoulder. "It's been many years, but I'm glad you haven't forgotten our discussion. Tonight, I will tell you where it may be hidden."

# CHAPTER 45

The imposing Professor Taube sat erect and focused his magnetic blue eyes on Mayer. "When I was a boy, my family lived in France. A few days before my thirteenth birthday, my father took me to the great Gothic cathedral at Chartres. The graceful soaring towers and extraordinary luminescent stained glass windows were impressive. However, what awed me most was a small stone relief carving on a portal column of the Gate of the Initiates. It depicted the Israelites transporting the Ark of the Covenant.

"I recall asking my father how an important Jewish symbol could be found on a Christian Church. His response surprised me."

"What did he say?"

"He told me the architects of Chartres and the other great Christian cathedrals scattered throughout Europe relied on ancient Egyptian and Greek architectural principles used by the architect and builder of King Solomon's Temple and the first Grand Master of Freemasonry, Hiram Abif."

Mayer looked puzzled. "I don't understand. The architects of Christian churches in Europe used the same architectural principles as the architect of Solomon's Temple?"

"Yes. Hidden for over a thousand years in secret vaults below the Temple Mount, the ancient architectural manuscripts, unearthed by Templar Knights after the first Crusade, were secretly moved to Europe. Relying on the manuscripts, the Templars created throughout Europe hundreds of inspiring lofty churches noted for their luminescent stained glass windows. The small stone relief carving on the portal column commemorates the link between the Templar Knights—the Children of Solomon—and their Judaic ancestors. Since my visit to Chartres, I have been fascinated by the Judaic symbolism surrounding the Ark."

Mayer stroked his beard, captivated by the narrative.

Taube continued. "As you may recall, the Bible refers to the Prophet Jeremiah, sometime before the Babylonians sacked the Jerusalem Temple in 597 B.C., of removing the Ark from the Temple and hiding it in a secret cave at the base of a mountain referred to as the "Sacred Mountain of God." For many years, I pored over records in the National Library, the Shrine of the Book, as well as countless other libraries and historical journals."

Pausing for a moment, Taube sipped from his wine glass. Then setting the glass down, he said, "I couldn't find any significant information relating to the disappearance of the Ark, but quite by chance while conducting research at the National Library, I came across the journal of Johann J. Burckhardt. In it, the 19th century Swiss explorer mentioned the name Ralph de Sudeley."

"I remember your mentioning his name some time ago."

Taube smiled and continued. "An English Templar Knight and leader of a Crusader garrison stationed near the ruined city of Petra around 1190 A.D., de Sudeley is said to have unearthed a golden chest fitting the description of the Ark in a cave at the base of a mountain the Bedouin referred to as Jebel Madhbah, the Mountain of God."

"Have you been to Jebel Madhbah?"

Taube nodded. "I have, and the stone altar at the summit of the mountain strongly resembles the biblical description of the mountain upon which God presented Moses with the Ten Commandments."

Mayer's face flushed with excitement. "You mean, Mt. Sinai?"

"Yes. The mountain archeologists have long searched for the real Mt. Sinai. I believe when the Templar Knight returned to England in 1189, he transported several large wooden crates containing a sizeable quantity of valuable Christian holy relics and the Ark.

"Though he sold many of the holy relics at considerable profit, he retained the Ark and buried it in a vault on his estate in Herdewyke. There it remained until, upon his death, his grandson, a Templar Knight, moved the Ark to the Templar Abbey of Kilwinning in Scotland for safekeeping. In the abbey, protected by Templar Knights and their descendants the Freemasons, it stayed for over 200 years. Then, in 1146 A.D., it was secretly transferred to the custody of Sir William St. Clair of Rosslyn."

Mayer looked perplexed. "St. Clair . . . Who is he?"

Taube threw his head back and gave a knowing smile. "Someone, who I assure you, is quite important to us. A wealthy aristocratic and Grand Commander of Scottish Freemasons, Sir William St. Clair was a direct descendant of the Crusader Knight, Baron Henri St. Clair of Rosslyn whose niece, Catherine St. Clair, married a founder of the Knights Templar, Hugues de Payen. St. Clair believed a mystical connection existed between the Templar Knights and the Ark of the Covenant, and so he embraced the idea of eternally protecting the Ark within the walls of Rosslyn Chapel."

Taube stood and gazed into the star-filled Mediterranean sky. Slowly turning, he faced Mayer. "Within the chambers below Rosslyn Chapel are several large wooden chests. They are of great interest to us. One chest, we think, contains a copper scroll larger and more detailed than the copper scroll found with the Dead Sea Scrolls at Qumran."

Mesmerized, Mayer listened in silence.

"In other chests are the secret scrolls of the Jerusalem Nazarene Church written by Jesus Christ and his brother James. The documents, discovered by the Templars, describe Christ as a leader of a Jewish movement opposed to the despotic rule of the Romans and their puppet King Herod Antipas. Contrary to Catholic Church dogma, the documents in Christ's own hand confirm that he never proclaimed himself a deity, but rather a Jewish leader who, in following the law of the Torah, served God and loved and conceived three children with Mary Magdalene."

"I'm not surprised Christ fathered several children," Mayer said, the edge of his mouth forming a sly smile. "After all, Christ was a Jew and Jewish law dictates a man shall not waste his seed."

Taube laughed. "You're right, but what you probably don't know is how Christianity began."

"Wasn't it started by Christ, and then continued by his disciples?"

Taube shook his head. "It may surprise you, Mayer, but that's not how Christianity began. A former Jewish priest in Herod's Temple founded Christianity. His name was Saul of Tarsus. Sometime after Christ was killed by the Romans, disillusioned with the corruption in Herod's Temple, he left Jerusalem and changed his name to Paul."

"Oh, yes. I've heard his name. Catholics refer to him as Saint Paul, but I didn't know he'd been a Jewish priest." Mayer looked puzzled. "Was he one of Christ's Apostles?"

"No, and though he never met Christ, he referred to himself as the 13th Apostle. In a dream Paul had, he said Jesus told him the time for the Jewish religion had ended and that he should organize a new religion. Paul even invented a new name for it—Christianity. It was based on the Greek name he created and added to Jesus name—Christus, or as we know it today, Jesus Christ."

"So that's how Christianity began."

"Not quite."

"What do you mean?

A subtle smile on his face, Taube replied, "Do you recall your initiation as an Essene member?"

Mayer threw up his hands. "Do I? I'll never forget it. I thought I was going to die when they lowered me into the cold crypt. Only when they raised me did I realize it was just a ritual."

"The symbolic death and resurrection ritual you experienced was an important part of the initiation ceremony practiced by our ancestors, the Essenes of Qumran. Somehow, Paul, a man who was never an Essene or ever visited Qumran, applied our symbolic initiation ritual to the death and subsequent resurrection of a man he named Jesus Christ. Now Mayer—you know the true origin of the Catholic Church."

Mayer shook his head. "Unbelievable."

"To protect the Templar legacy, the treasures, and the secret Nazarene scrolls they brought from Jerusalem, St. Clair commissioned the building of a special multi-layered underground structure within Rosslyn Chapel."

Taube went on. "The Ark of the Covenant has remained there for over 500 years in a hidden chamber below the main chapel. Ironically, although the exterior of the chapel relies heavily on flying buttresses and gargoyles in the medieval Gothic church style, St. Clair never intended Rosslyn Chapel serve as a Christian church.

"Within its walls, an exact replica of the interior of Herod's Jerusalem Temple, is the traditional Judaic priestly pillar of Jachin and the kingly pillar of Boaz. Carved on the interior pillars, walls and ceiling of the Chapel are Judaic, Celtic and Scandinavian symbols. Except for the stained glass windows added in the 19th century, conspicuously absent are any Christian symbolisms."

"Have you been to Rosslyn Chapel?"

"I've made several trips with a surveillance team. Using thermal imaging equipment, we secretly photographed and mapped every inch of the chapel's interior and exterior including the chapel's foundation and the below ground chambers."

Now on the edge of his chair, Mayer asked in an excited tone, "Do you intend to recover the Ark from Rosslyn Chapel?"

A determined look on his face, Taube replied, "With God's blessings, we will recover the Ark and return it to the Temple Mount."

Raising his hand, he motioned to Mayer. "There's something else I want you to see. Follow me."

# CHAPTER 46

A mirror of Taube's life-long interest in Judaic history and archeological research, his study was crammed with a sizeable collection of Judaic and archeological books, charts, and maps. On one wall hung a framed photograph of Colonel Taube and the former Chief of the Israel Defense Forces and noted Dead Sea Scrolls scholar, Lieutenant General Yigael Yadin. On another wall was a framed photograph of Professor Taube and several of his students at the Essene settlement excavation site in Qumran.

With Mayer looking on, Taube pulled a topographical map from a filing cabinet, unfolded it on his desk, and pointed with a pencil to a highlighted area of the map. "This is an aerial view of Rosslyn Chapel and the surrounding countryside."

Taube tacked four 8 x 10 photographs to a corkboard and pointed to the first one. "This is a partial view of the interior of the Chapel. Of primary interest to us is the Sacristy. Below its tiled floor is a concealed freestanding 30-foot-high structure. Access to the narrow stone staircases leading to the floors below requires the release of a series of keystones."

Taube pointed to the second photograph. "This section is part of the lower chamber. It's built partially over a deep pit and is particularly tricky to access. The weight of one person could cause the counterbalanced floor to tip and result in everything on the floor, including the Ark, to slide into the pit."

Mayer studied the photograph, then shook his head. "It seems impossible."

"It's risky, but it's feasible. Although the underground structure is cleverly protected with booby traps and a water reservoir that could flood the chambers, we think we can safely retrieve the Ark. Using a computer generated model our engineers have devised a method of entry which will use specially designed equipment to neutralize the booby traps and prevent collapse of the structure."

Taube pointed to the third photograph. It showed the image of a tall Templar Knight in full body armor and a cloak emblazoned with a splayed red cross. "He appears to fit the description of Sir William St. Clair. The other knights are probably his father Henry, second Prince of Orkney who Sir William succeeded, his grandfather, and another St. Clair family member."

Referring to another image on the same photograph, Taube said, "The first trunk probably contains the original copper scroll written by the Essenes and hidden below the Temple Mount around 68 A.D. The scroll, unearthed by Templar Knights, members of the secret Priory of the Scion, was discovered in a vault beneath the temple mount. It documented the location of ancient Judaic manuscripts, long lost Egyptian and Greek geometry codes, and a sizeable quantity of gold bullion."

Mayer nodded. "Now I understand what you meant when you referred to the Templar Knights earlier."

Shifting his focus, Taube directed Mayer's attention to the fourth photograph. "These trunks contain the diaries, journals, and records of the Nazarene Jerusalem Church. They were unearthed by the Templar Knights who uncovered the copper scroll. Written in the hand of Jesus Christ and his brother James, they reinforce the Templar belief—Christ was a human and not, as professed by the Catholic Church, a deity."

Taube went on. "Believing one day the world would be ready for the truth long suppressed by the Catholic Church, Sir William St. Claire devised an ingenious plan to protect the valuable Nazarene Church documents in a secret chamber below Rosslyn Chapel. As with the Templars who considered the Jesus of Nazareth documents their greatest treasure, we think the manuscripts can be of value to us as well.

"Now, Mayer, here's the best part." Taube pointed to the fourth photograph. It showed an image of a large wooden trunk. "That, we believe, contains our primary objective—the Ark of the Covenant."

Mayer frowned. "How can you be sure? To me it looks like a large wooden trunk."

"It does, but after considerable analysis, we're confident this trunk contains the Ark of the Covenant."

His heart beating rapidly, drops of perspiration visible on his forehead trickled through Mayer's beard. Wiping the perspiration from his forehead with a handkerchief, he turned his eyes to Taube. "I'm amazed by what you have uncovered, but there is something I have been meaning to ask you for some time."

"What is it?" Taube asked, arching an eyebrow.

"I understand the power of the Ark protected the Israelites in battle, but how did it work?"

"I'll show you." Taube withdrew a folder from a black filing cabinet and removed an artist's rendering of the Ark of the Covenant. "The Ark behaved much like a capacitor would today."

"What's a capacitor?"

"Are you familiar with a defibrillator?"

"Sure. A defibrillator is used to resuscitate people who've had a heart attack."

Taube nodded. "A defibrillator contains a cylinder-like object called a capacitor. It stores and increases the voltage of energy generated by the defibrillator battery. When triggered, the defibrillator releases a jolt of high voltage energy stored in the capacitor to restart the heart. In a similar way, lighting and other electrical sources were attracted to the Ark's gold encased arenite sandstone.

"The Ark, like a geoplasmic generator, creates electrical energy and stores the energy for later use, but the generated energy can become highly volatile. That explains the Bible references to people who died instantly when they inadvertently touched the Ark. We also believe the Ark's stored energy, triggered by a signal generated and transmitted by the polished stones worn on the vest of the high priest, protected the Israelites from their enemies during their forty-year desert exile."

Mayer's face flushed with excitement. "Do think we'll use it as a weapon?"

Taube shook his head and laughed. "No, I don't think so. We have many other powerful modern weapons, but the Ark is a great symbol of our covenant with God and a powerful tool we can use to intimidate our enemies. Remember, the plans for the Ark's construction, referred to in the Bible, were given to Moses by God on Mt. Sinai along with the stone tablets inscribed with the Ten Commandments."

"When do you plan on recovering the Ark?"

"Soon after the Temple Mount is retaken, a new temple will rise on the Temple Mount. Then we'll recover the Ark. In the meantime, the date for the launch of 'The Event' has been set."

The next morning, Mayer traveled by car with Taube to Bat Yam. There they joined their fellow Essene brothers in an all day conclave at the Essene command center concealed within the Bobov Yeshiva compound. Mayer returned to Taube's home after midnight. Though physically tired, he felt elated. As he drifted off to sleep, he envisioned the important role he would play in the new Israeli government.

# CHAPTER 47

Before Mayer returned to New York, he visited the most sacred symbol of the Jewish faith, the Western Wall. At 7:20 a.m. the area in front of the Wall almost deserted, he recited his morning prayers. When he finished, a large white prayer shawl still draped over his head, he stepped back several paces and stared up at the gleaming Golden Dome of the Rock perched on the Temple Mount.

As he grasped the gold pendant inscribed with the three blue rectangular concentric lines he wore suspended from his neck, he thought of his first visit to Jerusalem. Then a young yeshiva student, he recalled one of his teachers, an old grey-bearded rabbi, referring to the biblical prophecy of Jeremiah 23:3-6. "A Messiah," he had said, "will one day appear and lead the chosen people of Israel in the building of a new temple to house the most mysterious icon of the Jewish faith and the only physical manifestation of God on earth—the Ark of the Covenant."

Mayer retrieved a folded slip of paper from his jacket pocket. Bowing his head reverently, he murmured a prayer for God to bless and empower the Essene Brotherhood's mission, then slipped the encoded message into a crevice in the ancient wall.

Soon, he thought, a rush of adrenaline surging through his body, only one building will stand on the Temple Mount, the house of Yahweh. Energized, he placed his prayer shawl in a velvet bag, turned away from the Wall, and headed toward the Jewish Quarter.

CHAPTER **48**

At 6:50 p.m., less than an hour after he spoke with McClure, Davidov called the office of the head of airport security at Tel Aviv's Ben Gurion International Airport, Zvi Landau. His assistant indicated his boss had gone to the airport operations center, but sensitive to a call from a high-ranking intelligence officer, he attempted to be helpful. "Is there anything I can do?"

"No," Davidov replied tersely, "I'll try to reach him on his cell phone."

Already late for a diplomatic dinner, Davidov dialed Landau's cell number. The two men knew each other well. Landau had previously served as a major in an IDF unit commanded by Davidov during the 1973 Yom Kippur War.

"Shalom, Zvi, it's Ari Davidov. I need your help; I don't have much time to talk."

Though he'd had a long demanding day, Landau replied in a steady voice, "How can I help you?"

"I want you to begin inspecting the luggage of all passengers arriving from the United States or Canada."

"We already conduct inspections, at least on a selective basis."

"I know you do, but for the next several weeks, I want a thorough inspection of all arriving passengers' luggage. I'm particularly interested in the luggage of Hasidic passengers."

Surprise reflected in the tone of his voice, Landau repeated, "Hasidic passengers?"

"Yes, that's what I said."

Landau held his cell phone to his ear and scanned the arriving aircraft schedule. "There's an El Al flight arriving from New York tomorrow morning and one from Toronto in the afternoon."

"Good. That's a start."

"We can check every arriving passenger, but I'll need additional personnel."

"Whatever it takes, you have my authorization."

"Is there anything we should be on alert for?"

"I'm especially interested in passengers carrying large amounts of U.S. dollars or English pounds. Call me if you find anything suspicious."

"I will."

"One other thing you should be aware of, Zvi. As this could be a national security issue, I want you to personally handle this matter."

"I understand. Shalom."

The next morning, at one minute past eight, Davidov initiated a call to Yaakov Cohen, Director of the Israeli Security Service, the Shin Bet.

Recognizing the caller's ID, Cohen lifted the telephone handset on the second ring.

"Shalom, Ari. So for what do I owe the honor of a call at this early hour?"

"I need some information."

"Tell me what you want."

Davidov proceeded to brief Cohen on the information he had received a day earlier from Harry McClure.

Typical of the methodology he followed, Cohen probed for additional information. "Who are we dealing with?"

"His name is Mayer Rubin. He's a U.S. citizen and lives in the Boro Park Hasidic community in Brooklyn, NY."

"Oh yes, I know the community. They're religious fanatics."

"Mr. Rubin is the head of a group that's been manipulating the shares of companies listed on NASDAQ for many years. He's of special interest to us since most of the profits from the illegal transactions are channeled to Israeli bank accounts."

"Do you know why?"

"No, I don't, but I'm concerned. There's a lot of money involved." Davidov read off a list of banks, names, and account numbers. "I want to know the owner and signatures on each account, amounts and dates of transfers, and the amount currently in each account."

"Can I get a copy of the list?"

"I'll have Naomi fax it to you."

"We have excellent contacts at all of the banks, but as you know, they are usually uncooperative when it comes to releasing customer account information."

"I don't care, Yaakov. We may be dealing with a major security issue. I need this information without delay."

"You'll have it within a few days. Shalom."

# CHAPTER **49**

**M**ax read the note his assistant handed him, then glanced at the faces of his marketing team assembled around the conference table. "I've got a call I need to take. I'll be back shortly." Closing the door to his office behind him, he reached for the telephone on his desk.

"Good morning, Stan."

"I've got to catch a flight in two hours, so let me get right to the point," Jacob replied.

Max pressed the phone to his ear. "Sure, go ahead."

"After our meeting at Harry's office, I prepared and sent to the Justice Department a brief detailing Mayer Rubin and Mark Federman's alleged manipulation, illegal trading, and profiting from the sale of NovoMed stock and 10 other NASDAQ companies.

"It appears my brief could not have come at a better time. An earlier Justice Department case against Mayer Rubin is stalled in federal court, so they've requested a special grand jury to examine the material I forwarded to them. More than likely, the grand jury will convene within three weeks." Jacob paused. "Max, are you willing to testify?"

"Just tell me when. I'll be there."

"Before you meet with the grand jury, you can expect a call from FBI Special Agent Jack Molloy.

"How should I answer his questions?"

"Tell him exactly what you have told me. Be candid and truthful. Remember you are not the target of their investigation."

"I understand."

"There's one other issue. As you know, Harry discussed Mayer Rubin's money laundering scheme with his contact in the Israeli government."

"Yes, I am aware of his discussion."

"The outcome of the Israeli investigation could have a bearing on the federal case we are building against Rubin, Federman, and their co-conspirators. In light of the sensitive nature of the investigation, I hope you don't mind a little lawyerly advice."

"No, I don't."

"Be especially careful and don't discuss the ongoing investigation with anyone. If word leaks, it could tip our hand."

"Don't worry. I'll be careful."

"I'll be in touch."

A week later, Max met with FBI Special Agent Jack Molloy. Guided by Jacob's advice, he fully cooperated with the FBI and turned over copies of all NovoMed files pertaining to Mayer Rubin.

# CHAPTER 50

Z vi Landau's easygoing wife often teased, "You're so precise, Zvi. Everything in your life has to be just right."

As the Director of Security at Ben Gurion International Airport, Landau's obsession with detail served him well. Born and raised in Israel, a Sabra, he had earned an advanced degree in Semitic languages from Hebrew University in Jerusalem.

Fluent in eight languages, including Hebrew, Yiddish, Arabic, French and English, he possessed an uncanny ability to identify terrorists, smugglers, and others seeking unlawful entry into Israel. Trained to know that dialects and speech patterns provide insights into an individual's identity, he developed a knack for disarming arriving and departing passengers by conversing with them in their native tongues.

Similar to much of Israel's Jewish population, though he believed in God, Landau showed little interest in orthodox religious practices. Instead, he identified with the more contemporary beliefs and practices of Israel's reform Jewish population.

When one of the agents Landau had briefed earlier in the day on the new airport screening procedures called to say he had detained a man he wanted to question further, he quickly responded. The customs agent had uncovered two manila envelopes containing 500 U.S. $100 bills wrapped in newspaper in a black travel bag.

The agent stared at the elderly white-bearded Hasidic man who had arrived 30 minutes earlier on an El Al flight from New York. "You're carrying a lot of money in your bag, Mr. Frankel."

Frankel shrugged. "I don't know how it got there."

"You don't know?" The skeptical customs agent scowled. "No, I don't."

"Okay, then you'll have to come with me." He escorted Frankel into a private interrogation room and motioned to a wooden chair behind a bare wooden table. "Sit down."

A few minutes later a sandy-haired, broad-shouldered man dressed in a white open-collared shirt and dark trousers entered the interrogation room and introduced himself in Yiddish. "My name is Zvi Landau."

Before he initiated a rapid series of insightful questions, Landau offered Frankel a bottle of water. Frankel reached for the bottle, removed the cap, and proceeded to quench his thirst. Satisfied, he gingerly set the empty bottle on the table in front of him. Slowly nodding, he thanked Landau in Yiddish.

"Now Mr. Frankel, I'd like to ask you a few questions. First, are you originally from Warsaw?"

Landau's question surprised Frankel. Focusing his deep-set brown eyes on Landau, he replied, "I lived near Warsaw until the Nazis arrested my entire family and shipped us to Auschwitz." Lowering his eyes, he inhaled deeply. Then he lifted his gaze and asked in a cautious tone, "May I ask you a question, Mr. Landau?"

"Sure."

"How did you know I was from Warsaw?"

Landau smiled. "Before the war, my family lived near Warsaw. The few family members still surviving speak Yiddish with the same accent as yours."

Frankel heaved a sigh. "I guess I'm in a lot of trouble?"

"You could be, if you don't tell me the truth."

Fear registered on Frankel's face. *How I can betray a fellow Hasid?* Folding his hands, he stared at Frankel for several seconds.

Then, in a low voice, he said, "A member of the Hasidic community in Boro Park, Brooklyn requested I deliver a parcel to Israel."

"For what purpose?"

"He told me it was to help bring Hasidic Jews living in Russia to Israel. For my services, I received a round trip ticket to Israel and two thousand dollars in cash." His eyes filled with emotion, Frankel continued, "You see, Mr. Landau, I've always wanted to pray at the Wall before I die."

"I understand, Mr. Frankel, but I need to know the name of the person who asked you to deliver the parcel."

Frankel placed his hand over his mouth and lowered his head.

Landau sensed Frankel was close to revealing the name he wanted, so he increased the intensity of his questioning. "Let me remind you, Mr. Frankel . . ." He paused. "You're in serious trouble and could go jail for a long time."

The thought of prison was more than Frankel could bear. Raising his head, he stared fearfully at Landau. Then he blurted, "His name is Mayer Rubin."

Landau made a note on his pad. "And where were you instructed to deliver the money?"

"To a bank in Tel Aviv."

"Which bank?"

"I was given the name of Bank Leumi and an account number. I was told to take the money to the bank." Frankel shrugged. "That's all I know." Looking tired and frightened, he added, "Please, I beg that you believe me."

"I do, Mr. Frankel," Landau replied in a kind voice. "You don't have to be afraid. We're going to ask you to stay with us for a few days, but no harm will come to you."

Frankel clutched his chest and drew a long sigh of relief. "Thank you, Mr. Landau. After what I've been through, I don't think I could endure prison again."

Landau again scanned the face of the old Hasidic man sitting across the table. His bearded face and dark expressive eyes reminded him of a photograph he'd seen of one of his father's brothers, his uncle who had perished in the Holocaust. Though he never allowed his personal feelings to stand in the way of carrying out his professional duties, interrogating Frankel had troubled him.

Landau rose from his chair and walked around the table to where Frankel sat hunched in a rigid wooden chair. Gently placing his arm over his shoulder, he said in an empathetic tone, "Mr. Frankel, don't worry. I promise, no one will hurt you."

Frankel looked up and gazed motionless into Landau's blue eyes. A moment later the frightened expression on his face faded and his lips parted. "I believe you, Mr. Landau. Thank you."

# CHAPTER 51

A Bearded middle-aged man, with a characteristic Hasidic wide-brimmed black hat covering his head mingled among a group of other Hasidic men. Twenty minutes earlier, he had arrived at Ben Gurion International Airport on a flight from Toronto, Canada. Well known to Israeli customs agents, a frequent traveler to Israel, Shmuel Kaplan had never encountered any delay passing through airport customs inspection.

This trip was different. "Why are you interrogating me? I'm not a terrorist," Kaplan complained.

The customs agent gave a polite smile. "Please open your carry-on bag, Mr. Kaplan."

"Sure," Kaplan replied, his tone indignant.

The agent carefully looked through the carry-on bag. "That's fine. Now unzip your luggage."

Kaplan attempted to convey the impression that he had nothing to hide by unzipping the large black suitcase and laying it flat on the counter in front of the customs agent. The agent, carefully probing with both hands, first examined the contents on the left side of the case. Then he returned the contents to their original state and moved on to examining the right side of the suitcase.

When the agent placed his hands deep inside the case, he noticed the depth of the interior did not match the depth of the exterior. While he methodically removed each item of clothing, personal items, and prayer books from the open suitcase, he observed Kaplan's facial expression and body language.

"How do I open this compartment, Mr. Kaplan?"

His arms crossed against his chest, Kaplan's face tightened as he watched the customs agent open a pocketknife.

Spontaneously, Kaplan cried out, "Don't cut it. I'll open it for you."

Kaplan pulled a small ring concealed in the interior of the case. It released a spring-loaded hinge on the false bottom that revealed a hidden compartment. Within the compartment the customs agent viewed twenty foam compartments. Each compartment contained a neatly wrapped stack of crisp U.S. $100 bills.

Kaplan watched in silence as the customs agent picked up one of the stacks, removed the paper wrapper, and slowly counted one hundred bills equaling $10,000. Raising his head, the agent looked at Kaplan intently. "I assume the other stacks contain the same amounts of money?"

Kaplan stared at the agent, but didn't reply.

"There's a lot of money here," the agent snapped. Is it yours?"

"No. It's not mine."

"Then who does the money belong to?"

Kaplan avoided answering the question. He lowered his head and, as though suddenly transported into a trance like state, began to pray.

Undeterred, the customs agent waited until Kaplan had finished praying and regained his composure. "Now, Mr. Kaplan. Who gave you the money hidden in your luggage?"

Kaplan remained silent.

"You leave me no choice but to detain you." Motioning to several other agents who had surrounded Kaplan, he ordered, "Take him to room seven."

A minute later, the agent reached for his cell phone and called Landau. "I've detained a Hasidic man who arrived less than an hour ago on a flight from Toronto. He's carrying a large sum of U.S. currency and refuses to talk."

"I'll be over shortly."

For several hours, Landau interrogated Kaplan. Speaking in English, Kaplan revealed he was originally from New York. "My parents are Holocaust survivors who moved to Toronto when I was fourteen." Married and the father of three boys,

Kaplan lived in an affluent suburb of Toronto and traveled to Israel several times a year on business.

"What kind of business are you in, Mr. Kaplan?"

"I'm a diamond merchant."

Landau switched to Yiddish and confronted Kaplan in a harsh tone. "Is the money we found in your suitcase for one your clients?"

With beads of perspiration forming on his brow, Kaplan replied, "No," but refused to offer any further explanation.

Then, Mr. Kaplan, you'll be staying with us tonight."

Led to a private detention cell by a security guard, Kaplan was, to his dismay, required to remove all of his clothing and submit to a humiliating body search.

The guard pointed to the gold pendant inscribed with three rectangular concentric cobalt blue lines Kaplan wore on a gold chain around his neck. "Kindly remove the pendant and give it to me. It will be returned when you are released."

Kaplan tightly clutched the pendant with his right hand and shouted an obscenity at the guard.

Only after the guard threatened, "If you don't hand the pendant over to me, I'll rip it off your neck," did Kaplan reluctantly comply.

Alone in his cell, Kaplan was unaware a hidden camera and a microphone monitored his every movement and sound. Exhausted from the long flight and hours of interrogation, he fell asleep on a narrow metal cot.

A few minutes later, Landau called Davidov and gave him an update. "I'm sure we'll identify the intended recipient of the money found in Mr. Kaplan's luggage, but I'm perplexed by the unusual gold pendant he was wearing. It's inscribed with three rectangular concentric blue lines. He was reluctant to surrender it. Though he vehemently denied it, the gold pendant is obviously of great value to him."

Intrigued, Davidov requested Landau send the pendant to his office for evaluation. "Keep up the pressure and call me as soon as you have anything new to report."

# CHAPTER 52

When Kaplan awoke at 5:30 the next morning, he was permitted to pray and put on tefillin. After a light breakfast, a guard escorted him to a windowless room and seated him on a bare wooden chair. A few minutes later, Landau strode into the room.

"How are you, Mr. Kaplan?"

"I'm alright," Kaplan replied, his tone unemotional.

"Good, let's continue where we left off last night. I should warn you, we'll be seeing a lot of each other until you tell me the truth."

Kaplan gave Landau a contemptuous stare. "You are treating me like I'm a terrorist."

Landau smiled. "Are you, Mr. Kaplan?"

Kaplan's face flushed. "No. I'm only an Orthodox Jew committed to upholding our biblical covenant with God."

Landau's instincts, reinforced by Kaplan's sudden burst of anger, told him he was making progress. Locking his eyes on Kaplan, he asked, "What does God expect of you?"

Before he replied, Kaplan pondered Landau's question. "He expects total commitment to the fulfillment of our sacred covenant with him."

Landau pressed. "So Mr. Kaplan, is that the purpose of the money found in your suitcase?" Noting Kaplan's blank stare, Landau decided to shift to a new line of questions. "Can you tell me what the three blue concentric lines inscribed on the pendant you were wearing around your neck signify?"

Kaplan pursed his lips. "It's a good luck charm."

"A good luck charm?" Landau repeated. "Who gave you the pendant?"

Kaplan again lowered his eyes. "My father-in-law before he passed away. It had been in his family for a long time."

Convinced Kaplan was lying, Landau was ready to fire off another round of questions when his cell phone vibrated. Glancing at the phone's screen, he recognized Davidov's number.

"Excuse me Mr. Kaplan, I'll be right back. I hope by the time I return your memory is refreshed."

Davidov got right to the point. "The account number the elderly Hasidic man gave you is in the name of a yeshiva in Jerusalem run by a Hasidic rabbi. We're running a check on him and his yeshiva. In the meantime, ask Mr. Kaplan if he knows a Rabbi Katz."

"Okay. I'll pose that question to him."

Landau returned to the interrogation room and fixed his gaze on a somber faced Kaplan. "Is there anything more you want tell me?"

Kaplan gave a defiant smile. "No I've told you all I know."

For several minutes, the only sound in the room was the drone emanating from an overhead fan. While he slowly sipped coffee from a paper cup, Landau closely observed Kaplan's facial expression. Setting his cup down, he then began a new line of questioning in Yiddish. "Do you know a Rabbi Katz?"

The defiant smile on Kaplan's face suddenly evaporated.

Landau knew he had hit a nerve. *It's time to increase the pressure.* "Once again, Mr. Kaplan, do you know Rabbi Katz?"

"Yes. I've met him once or twice. He teaches classes on Torah and the Talmud."

"Would you say you know him well?"

"No, not well."

"Is the money in your suitcase meant for him or his yeshiva?"

"No," Kaplan replied adamantly.

Landau persisted. "Are you sure Mr. Kaplan that none of the money we discovered hidden in your suitcase is for Rabbi Katz?"

Now visibly agitated, Kaplan pointed his index finger at Landau and shouted, "I told you. The money is not for Rabbi Katz."

Landau raised his voice, almost shouting. "If the money isn't for Rabbi Katz, then who is it intended for?"

Kaplan responded with an icy stare.

"Then, Mr. Kaplan, you leave me no choice. You'll be returned to your cell and shall remain there until you are ready to tell me the truth."

Landau signaled a security guard standing in the corner of the room. "Please take Mr. Kaplan back to his cell." The guard nodded and escorted Kaplan out of the room.

Several minutes later, Landau was again on the phone with Davidov. "How is the interrogation going?" Davidov asked.

"His veneer is beginning to crack, but he's very crafty. I suspect this is not the first time he illegally transported money into Israel."

"Have you run a check on earlier passenger flight records from North America?"

"We have. In fact, Mr. Kaplan has been to Israel, arriving from either New York or Toronto, seven times in the last two years. Though he denies any of the money is destined for Rabbi Katz, I have a hunch based on how agitated he became when I asked about him that their relationship is more than casual."

"What about Mr. Frankel?"

"I'm of the opinion he knows nothing about Rabbi Katz. He's a kindly old man carrying around a lot of horrible memories, someone who has been badly exploited."

"Let me know if you pick up any other couriers or if Mr. Kaplan changes his mind and decides to talk. In the meantime, I'm expanding our investigation of Rabbi Katz and his yeshiva. There's much more we need to know about him and his organization. What we've uncovered might be just the tip of the iceberg."

# CHAPTER 53

Ariel Davidov sat six seats to the right of Israeli Prime Minister Yitzhak Shamir at a long conference table. The Prime Minister, eager to expand trade with Europe, was hosting a three-day high-level conference with senior officials of the Federal Republic of Germany and members of the Israeli Knesset.

Aware that her boss was anxiously awaiting a call from the head of the Shin Bet, Davidov's assistant, Naomi, silently delivered a note to him. *Mr. Cohen called. He said he has important information and wants to talk to you as soon as possible.* Pulling a pen from his suit pocket, Davidov scribbled a reply below the message and handed it to her. *Tell him I will call within the hour.* She scanned the note, nodded, then quietly exited.

Forty-five minutes later, Davidov excused himself, then walked down the hall to his office and dialed Cohen's private line. Cohen answered on the first ring.

"Shalom, Yaakov. I'm sorry I couldn't get to you sooner, but I've been in an all day meeting with the German Minister of Trade."

Cohen chuckled. "Oh, I know Ari how exciting those Germans can be."

"Anyway, what do you have for me?"

"We've checked the bank accounts from the list you faxed. At first, I couldn't believe the amounts, so I requested a recheck." Cohen paused. "The amounts passing through the accounts you sent me are staggering."

Davidov inhaled. "How much?"

"For the last five years the total is in excess of $300 million.

Stunned, Davidov raised his voice. "Are you sure?"

Yes, I'm positive—and there's probably more going back another five years. The accounts are in the name of Rabbi Katz or the yeshiva he runs in Jerusalem."

"Is the money currently in the accounts?"

"No. Within 90 days after deposit, the funds are withdrawn or transferred to a Swiss bank account."

"What do you think they're using the money for?"

"I can't imagine, but I think we need to know."

Davidov pressed the phone to his ear. "What do you propose?"

"I recall your mentioning this matter could affect our national security?"

"Yes, it could."

"Then under the circumstances, I would like your approval to enter and install bugs in Rabbi Katz's home and yeshiva. I can assure you my men will be discrete."

"Okay. You have my approval, but I don't want to read about your escapade in *The Jerusalem Post*."

"I understand. Leave it to me."

"How long will it take?"

"No more than a week."

"Keep me posted. Shalom."

# CHAPTER 54

Ariel Davidov was in a hurry. "Naomi, I want to send a fax to Harry McClure in New York right away."

Seated in front of Davidov's desk, she turned to a new page in her steno pad. "Alright, I'm ready."

> "Dear Harry,
>     An initial five-year review of the accounts you sent me indicates that large sums of U.S. currency were deposited into Israeli banks by Mayer Rubin and his agents. We have launched an aggressive investigation to determine the purpose of the funds. I expect additional information will be available early next week.
>
> Best regards,
> Ari"

Two hours later Naomi handed Davidov a fax from Harry McClure. It read:

*Dear Ari,*

*Thanks for the information. I thought you would like to know, a federal grand jury is convening next week in Brooklyn federal court. My source indicated that Mr. Rubin and his co-conspirators will, more than likely, be indicted on multiple federal charges. I'll keep you posted.*

*All the best,*
*Harry*

# CHAPTER 55

Roni Davidov believed the ritual of sharing the evening meal with her family played an important role in her children's well-being. In reality, however, Dr. Davidov, an obstetrician and gynecologist at the Hadassah Hospital in Jerusalem, and her husband each had demanding careers. Often, one or both of them was absent from dinner.

This Sunday, the Davidov family was enjoying a special dinner in celebration of their daughter's 14th birthday. Happy voices and laughter filled the room.

At ten minutes before seven, the telephone rang. A sudden silence fell over the room. "Should I get it, Mom?"

"Yes, Devorah."

Ariel Davidov hoped his wife wouldn't be called away for a medical emergency. A moment later, their daughter returned to the dining room. "It's for you Papa."

"Who is it?"

"It's Yaakov Cohen. He says it's important."

Davidov looked at his wife and sensed disappointment in her eyes. Though often called away on business, he was determined not to disappoint his family on his daughter's birthday.

Returning a few minutes later, he whispered in his wife's ear. "I won't be leaving until dinner is over and dessert is served." Grateful, she hugged him.

After the dinner plates were cleared, Roni Davidov placed a specially prepared birthday cake adorned with 14 candles on the dining room table. Eyeing the cake, her daughter Devorah took a deep breath and blew out all 14 candles. Reacting with joyous emotion each family member took their turn embracing her as the others applauded. After he enjoyed a slice of his daughter's birthday cake, Davidov glanced at his watch. *9:30. I'd better get going.*

Before leaving, he kissed and hugged his daughter. Then he placed his arms around his wife's shoulders and gazed into her eyes. "I've got an emergency, sweetheart. I'm going to my office and I'm not sure what time I'll be back. Don't wait up."

She planted a soft kiss on his lips, then whispered into his ear, "I love you, Ari. Be careful."

"I love you, too."

# CHAPTER 56

The uniformed security guard recognized the license plate on Davidov's black Mercedes, but, always on the alert for a possible security breach, he followed a strict prescribed protocol. Uzi submachine gun in hand, he cautiously observed the approaching car and waited for the driver to stop and roll down his window. Confirming Davidov's identity, he motioned for him to proceed to a secure underground garage.

As Davidov exited the elevator, another uniformed guard met him.

"Shalom, Mr. Davidov. Mr. Cohen is waiting in your office."

"How long has he been waiting?"

"About ten minutes."

Davidov nodded and headed down the hall to his office.

Yaakov Cohen, the Director of Shin Bet, the Israeli counter-intelligence and internal security service, his eyes fixed on the front door, waited anxiously in Davidov's reception room.

As the door opened, he sprang to his feet and feigned a smile. Greeted by Davidov with a quick nod, he followed his boss and settled into an upholstered chair facing Davidov's desk.

"Sorry I had to call you at home, Ari, but what we've uncovered couldn't wait until tomorrow."

Davidov leaned back in his chair and inhaled. "It's the nature of how we live in Israel. There's always a crisis. Tonight my family had gathered to celebrate my daughter's birthday and—" Sensing Cohen's anxiousness, Davidov abruptly stopped in the middle of his sentence. "It's alright Yaakov. I'm sure you have important information for me."

Cohen's eyes locked on Davidoff. "We have a major problem."

Detecting an unusual urgency in Cohen's voice, Davidov said, "Please continue."

"After we spoke last week, we set up a tap on Rabbi Jacob Katz's telephone. The rabbi, it seems, is a busy man. Since our surveillance began, he's had a lot of phone traffic. Nothing unusual, but he mentioned 'The Event' on two separate occasions."

Davidov raised his eyebrows. "Do you think it's some sort of code word?"

"It could be. When we discovered that he'd be staying with his family at Kirit Bobov for the Sabbath, we seized the opportunity to search his house and the adjoining yeshiva. Initially we found nothing suspicious. The house contained framed portraits of family members, Tzedek leaders, prayer books, a menorah, and Judaic religious material—the kind of things you would expect to find in the home of an orthodox rabbi."

As Davidov listened to Cohen, he thought, *The Shin Bet has uncovered a looming new threat to Israel's security.*

"Though on the surface everything appeared in order, my agents continued to probe. Searching through old Torah and Talmudic books on a heavy wooden bookcase, they noticed the left side of the bookcase was attached to the wall by a concealed hinge. Pulling the bookcase slightly back from the wall exposed a spring loaded catch. When they released the catch, the bookcase slowly swung away from the wall and revealed a padlocked heavy door.

"After picking the lock, my agents opened the door and turned on a light switch. Within the windowless room on a long table, they found a three-dimensional scaled diorama of Jerusalem. As they moved closer to the table, they noted a white marble building on the Temple Mount surrounded by three concentric rectangular walls."

Cohen reached into his attaché case and withdrew a packet of 8x10 photographs. "Take a look at these."

Davidov viewed the first photograph. "Am I looking at the Temple Mount?"

"You are."

"But all that I see is a single temple building surrounded by a walled courtyard."

"You're viewing a scale model rendering of Herod's Temple. A plaque written in ancient Hebrew attached to the side of the table referred to the temple as the Sanctuary of the Holy of the Holiest, where once again Yahweh will reside. It goes on to say, no other building shall ever again share the Temple Mount with the Temple of Yahweh."

"Do you mean they're planning to destroy the Dome of the Rock and the al-Aqsa Mosque?"

"That's their plan."

Davidov shook his head. "It's unbelievable. Now I understand the significance of the diorama your men discovered in Rabbi Katz's secret room."

Cohen's face tightened. "Ari, there's something else you need to know."

Stone-faced, Davidov motioned for Cohen to continue.

"In the same hidden room, we also found documents describing a secret society, the Essene Brotherhood. Their mission, believing a sacred relationship exists between God, the Chosen People, and the Temple Mount, is the restoration of Israel to its orthodox biblical roots. A gold plaque hanging on a wall adjacent to the model of the Temple Mount is inlaid with three rectangular concentric blue lines. It matches the pendant taken from Shmuel Kaplan."

"You know, Yaakov, you may have just solved the mystery of the three concentric lines we found on a card in the shirt pocket of slain Finance Minister, Uzi Kopelman. I have a feeling his death is somehow related to the Essene Brotherhood. Please continue."

"The symbol adopted by the Essene Brotherhood represents Herod's Temple and the three surrounding walls." Cohen inhaled. "Have you ever heard of the Essene Brotherhood?"

For a moment, Davidov reflected. "Aren't they the sect credited with authoring the Dead Sea Scrolls?"

Cohen nodded. "Yes. The Essenes were the secret sect the Romans annihilated because of their opposition to the rule of King Herod and later his son Antipas. Their belief in a Messianic prophecy may be the reason Rabbi Katz's group has adopted the Essene Brotherhood name."

"I wonder," Davidov asked, "are the Essenes related to the group that attempted to place a cornerstone on the Temple Mount last year?"

"I thought there might be a connection, so we checked them and every other known radical group, including fanatics like Yoel Lerner, the MIT trained mathematician who tried to blow up the Dome of the Rock, Yehuda Etzion's Jewish Underground, Gershon Salomon's Temple Mount Faithful, and the Kahane Chi, an offshoot of Rabbi Kahane's Kach organization."

Grim-faced, Cohen continued. "I am confident the Essene Brotherhood is a different group and far better organized and financed than any radical group we've previously encountered in Israel. We know from the documents we found, that they've stockpiled weapons and materials in secret underground warehouses scattered throughout Israel. The Essene Brotherhood believes Israel should be returned to an Orthodox Judaic state governed by the law of the Torah."

# CHAPTER 57

H is hands held in front of his face, the tips of his fingers touching, Davidov stared at Cohen. "I sense there's something else you want to tell me."

Cohen slowly nodded. "There is. We've also found the Essene Brotherhood manifesto for the reshaping and cleansing of Israel. It details their plan to demolish the Dome of the Rock and in its place construct a Judaic Temple."

Davidov didn't attempt to hide his frustration. In an angry voice he asked, "What else are they planning?"

Cohen sprang to his feet. His outstretched hands firmly gripping Davidov's desk, he stared into Davidov's eyes. "Listen carefully to me, Ari . . ." Pausing, he inhaled. "The Essene Brotherhood is planning to assassinate the Prime Minister and install a new government."

Stunned by the head of the Shin Bet's powerful statement, Davidov fired back, "Assassinate the Prime Minister?"

"That's their intention."

For a moment, a speechless Davidov stared at Cohen. Then he asked, "How many years have they been planning their conspiracy?"

"From the information we've gathered, it appears the Essene Brotherhood has been formulating their plans for over twenty five-years. The leader of the group, Rabbi Jacob Katz, traces his lineage back to the high priest of King Solomon's Temple."

"You mean he's a Golan Kohein?"

"Yes, the high priest who officiated at the ritual ceremonies in the first and second temples. We found a photograph of him wearing an elaborate ceremonial robe and hat."

"What else do we know about their operation?"

"In the filing cabinets we discovered detailed records of their membership. Mayer Rubin is a member. Recruited as a young Hasidic yeshiva student in 1967, he's a major fundraiser, but not the only one. There are other clandestine cells operating in North America and Europe. For many years, they've methodically recruited both Hasidic and non-Hasidic Orthodox Jews, highly respected members of the academic community, government officials, and several high ranking military officers."

Astonished, Davidov fired back, "There are high-ranking military men in his group?"

"Yes. Their members include two generals and three colonels, one of whom worked in my unit."

His face visibly strained, Davidov rose from his desk and eyed a wall map of Jerusalem. "So," he said, turning to Cohen, "they're planning to assassinate the Prime Minister, take over the government, and destroy the Dome of the Rock and the al-Aqsa Mosque?"

Cohen nodded. "That's their plan. Once they've cleared the Temple Mount of all Muslim buildings, they then intend to construct a new Grand Temple."

Cohen pointed to the photograph of the Temple Mount diorama. "The new temple will replicate Herod's Temple destroyed by the Romans in 70 A.D. The Ark of the Covenant, it appears, is an important Essene ritualistic symbol. One of their leaders, Professor Avraham Taube, a retired army colonel and now a Professor of History and Archeology at Hebrew University, seems to have discovered where the Ark may be hidden."

Davidov shook his head. "You know this whole business is beginning to sound like a movie I saw several years ago. Remember Raiders of the Lost Ark?" For the first time since their meeting began, both men briefly laughed.

"It may sound like a movie, Ari, but I'm convinced this is the real thing. My men also found detailed plans of a famous church in Scotland, Rosslyn Chapel. Confident the Ark is hidden in a secret chamber below the main chapel, the Essenes have developed an elaborate plan to recover and transport the Ark to Jerusalem."

"Do you realize, Yaakov, we may be dealing with an international crisis of enormous consequence? The secret radical group calling itself the Essene Brotherhood will, if we don't stop them, assassinate our Prime Minister, start a new war with the Muslims, and at the same time place Israel at risk of being condemned by the rest of the world."

Davidov thought for a moment. "This must be 'The Event' they've referred to. Do you have any idea of when they plan to launch their attack?"

"We've found a date circled in red on the wall calendar within the rabbi's secret room. The date coincides with the destruction of both the Solomon and Herod Temples."

Now furious, Davidov shouted, "Damn it! You mean Tisha B'Av? That's only two weeks from today."

"Yes, that's the date they've set to launch their surprise attack."

Locking his eyes on Cohen, Davidov struck his desk with a fisted hand. "We must stop them! The Essene Brotherhood can't destroy Israel. I'll meet with the Prime Minister in the morning and brief him on our discussion. He will, of course, want to know why your department failed to uncover the Essene Brotherhood conspiracy earlier."

Cohen groaned. "I'm sure he will. For now, you can assure him, we can stop the Essenes. It's not too late."

Davidov nodded, and then glanced at the time on his watch. "It's almost two. Let's go home and get some rest."

As they walked through the underground garage, Davidov suddenly stopped and turned to Cohen. "One last question. Do you think Rabbi Katz and his Essenes suspect we are onto their plans?"

Cohen gazed wearily at Davidov. "I'm confident they're unaware of our surveillance. Everything appears normal. 'The Event' launch date has not changed. It's still scheduled for the first day of Tisha B'Av, Sunday the 21st of July."

# CHAPTER 58

Noting the strained look on her boss's face, Naomi asked, "Is something wrong?"

Davidov snapped back, "We've got a new crisis. I need to meet with the Prime Minister as soon as possible. Tell his secretary it's an urgent matter."

Ten minutes later, Naomi returned. "The Prime Minister will see you at eleven, but I think I should warn you. He's having a bad day."

Davidoff nodded. "I understand."

Two minutes before eleven, he hurried down the corridor to the Prime Minister's office. The Prime Minister's secretary greeted him and motioned for him sit on a couch across from her desk. Eyeing her phone, she noted the lighted diodes, a moment earlier glowing, were off. She knew, if she had any chance of getting Davidov into the Prime Minister's office immediately, she'd have to act quickly. Springing from her

desk, she gave Davidov a quick glance. "I'll be right back."
Two minutes later, she reappeared and motioned with her
index finger in the direction of the Prime Minister's office.
"He'll see you now."

Davidov smiled appreciatively. "Thank you."

No stranger to crisis, Yitzhak Shamir's controversial career
spanned more than 50 years. A militant Zionist, he had earlier
in his career served his country as a soldier, espionage agent,
and member of the Knesset. Born in Poland, he emigrated to
Palestine in 1935. A short time later, he joined the Irgun Zvai
Leumi. An underground Jewish militia group, it opposed
British control of Palestine.

In 1940, when the Irgun divided into two groups, he sid-
ed with the more militant Lehl faction.  In secret, although
they were unsuccessful, the Lehl group contacted German
diplomats and proposed Jewish military action against the
British in return for the expulsion of Jews from Nazi-occupied
Europe to Palestine. Following distinguished service in
Mossad, Israel's secret intelligence service, he was elected to
the Knesset. Holding a narrow margin of victory, he was now
in his second term as Prime Minister.

As Davidov approached his desk, Shamir looked up from
the report he was reading.

"What a day, Ari. Members of my own party are mad at
me for proposing direct talks between Israel and her neighboring Arab States." Shamir waved his hand in the air. "Anyway,

what is it? I can tell something is bothering you. Is there a problem with Muslim terrorists?"

"No, Mr. Prime Minister. It's a much more serious matter."

"Alright, sit down and tell me what's so urgent." Glancing at the clock on his desk, he added, "I don't have a lot time. I'm due at a luncheon for visiting American rabbis at twelve-thirty."

"Mr. Prime Minister," his words carefully measured, Davidov said, "I'll try to summarize the recent events that prompted my request to meet with you today. It all began several months ago after the murder of Finance Minister, Uzi Kopelman."

The Prime Minister interrupted. "I've been meaning to ask how that investigation is going."

"When we discovered a blood-soaked card in the shirt pocket of Uzi Kopelman bearing the name M. Rubin, I decided to contact a trusted American friend in New York, Harry McClure. Mr. McClure is the head of an international security-consulting firm. We first met in 1972 when he was an American Naval Intelligence Officer stationed in Israel. During the planning of the Entebbe rescue operation, he provided us with high resolution U-2 aerial spy photographs of the Entebbe International Airport and communications jamming equipment."

As a former Mossad agent, Shamir appreciated the U.S. government's willingness to share intelligence information with Israel. Motioning with his hand, he signaled Davidov to continue.

"During the course of his investigation on our behalf, McClure uncovered Mayer Rubin. We now know that Mr. Rubin has been manipulating and profiting from illegal stock trading of publicly held technology companies in the United States. Of particular interest to us is that McClure's investigation revealed that much of the illegally generated money had been systematically transferred to Israeli banks."

Leaning forward, Shamir asked, "Who is this man, Mayer Rubin?"

"McClure identified him as a Hasid living in Boro Park, Brooklyn. Our airport flight records confirmed that he frequently travels between New York and Israel."

His hand supporting his chin, the Prime Minister asked, "Have you run across him before?"

"No, his name isn't in our database. Using the bank account information McClure supplied, I directed the Shin Bet to contact the named banks and inspect the listed accounts. I was shocked when Yaakov Cohen told me the size of the accounts."

His eyes widening, the Prime Minister asked, "How much money is involved?"

"Over a five-year period, the deposits totaled more than four hundred million U.S. dollars."

"That's a lot of money. What could they possibly be using it for?"

"That's what I wanted to know. So, when McClure informed me that Mr. Rubin regularly dispatched Hasidic couriers carrying concealed U.S. currency, I immediately alerted the head of airport security, Zvi Landau."

Shamir smiled. "Oh, yes, I know Zvi. I like him. He's clever and thorough."

Davidov nodded in agreement. "With Landau's help, we determined the money was destined for accounts controlled by a Rabbi Katz. The bank information he extracted from the couriers matched the bank information we had already secured. In a matter of days, the Shin Bet placed Rabbi Katz under surveillance and, unknown to him, gained access to his home in Jerusalem."

Shamir leaned back and listened in silence as Davidov continued.

"In the rabbi's house agents discovered a large bookcase concealing a locked door to a secret room. Within the secret room, on a table in the center of the room, was a diorama of the Temple Mount. But the only visible building on the Temple Mount was a scale model of Herod's Temple."

A puzzled look on his face, the Prime Minister asked, "What happened to the Dome of the Rock and the Al Aqsa Mosque?"

"That's what I wanted to know. A plan we found in the secret room describes how they intend to demolish the Muslim Holy building on the Temple Mount and forcibly drive all Muslims out of Israel. The Essenes believe their covenant with God empowers them to reclaim all biblical land God promised to their ancestors."

His jaw tightening, the Prime Minister clasped his hands together. "Is this the group, the Temple Faithful, who tried unsuccessfully to place a cornerstone on the Temple Mount earlier this year?"

"No, it isn't the same group. We've also ruled out all other known terrorist groups. This is a completely unknown organization."

"Do you know their name?"

"They call themselves the Essene Brotherhood or the Brothers of Light. Their name is derived from the monastic order of Essenes who once lived in Qumran and authored the Dead Sea Scrolls. This new group is highly organized, well financed, and includes Hasidic and non-Hasidic Orthodox Jews living in Israel and abroad, as well as members of the Knesset and several high ranking military officers."

In an angry tone, the Prime Minister exclaimed, "Members of the Knesset and high ranking military men. Are you sure?"

Davidov opened a manila folder and handed a single sheet marked TOP SECRET to the Prime Minister. He scanned the list. "I know these people. Some were members of the Irgun. Have they gone mad?" Visibly agitated, Shamir rose from his desk and began pacing the room. As he paced, his intercom buzzed. It was his secretary reminding him of his luncheon meeting.

"Esther, tell them I have the flu and apologize for me. Then call the Defense Minister and tell him he should attend the luncheon in my place. Also, find out where I can reach him and the other cabinet ministers later this afternoon. We may need to call an emergency meeting. Make certain I can reach all my ministers on short notice."

Shamir put down the phone and turned to Davidov. "Nature is calling. I'll be right back."

# CHAPTER 59

Shamir returned to his desk and motioned to Davidov. "Please continue."

"The Essene Brotherhood believes that Israel, unlike our present secular government, should be governed as it was in biblical times by the law of the Torah."

"Zealots," Shamir bellowed, "I remember when Israel declared its independence in 1948. Those crazy fanatics, all they wanted was a Jewish State governed by rabbis waiting for the Messiah to appear. Nothing else mattered."

Regaining his composure, Shamir's eyes narrowed. "Ari, is there anything else you haven't told me?"

"There is, Mr. Prime Minister."

"Ari, what the hell is it?"

"They intend to assassinate you."

Enraged, Shamir shouted, "Assassinate me?"

"Yes. We found the detailed plan. The news of the Temple Mount takeover will cause you to rush to Jerusalem. Along the route, your car will pass over a powerful bomb. The bomb will explode and kill you and your driver. Muslim terrorists will be blamed. It's a perfect scenario for the military to declare martial law and take over the government."

Stunned, Shamir lowered his eyes and placed his hand over his mouth. A few moments later, sitting upright, he clasped his hands together and calmly turned to Davidov. "I've been involved with conspirators like the Essenes before. They're not original, but they're cunning. When will it happen?"

"They intend to seize the Temple Mount and overthrow the government on the anniversary of the destruction of both Solomon's and Herod's temples."

"You mean Tisha B'Av?"

"Yes. The date is set for July 21st."

The Prime Minister glanced at the July calendar on his desk, then turned his eyes to Davidov. "There's not much time. Can we stop them?"

"I think we can. My plan is to conduct simultaneous raids on their command centers and apprehend all of their leaders before they can launch their conspiracy on Sunday July 21st. Secrecy is essential. There can be no leaks. Everything must appear as normal. As a precaution, from now on, I recommend you stay out of public view. When necessary, we'll have a double impersonate you."

Shamir took a deep breath and exhaled. "I understand."

"There's one other matter which requires your immediate attention. An American grand jury is meeting in federal court later this week. Mayer Rubin and his co-conspirators will more than likely be indicted. With your approval, I'm planning to fly to Washington, late tonight, to meet with the U.S. Secretary of State and the Attorney General. We need the Americans to postpone the announcement of the indictment of Mr. Rubin until after we can apprehend all of the Essene members involved in the plot in Israel."

A determined look in his eyes, Shamir waved his hand in the air. "You have my complete support. Do whatever it takes. I believe you know our ambassador to the United States, Zalman Shova."

"Yes, I know him."

"Tell him, on my authority, he is to provide you with any assistance you require. We don't always have the best relationship with the Americans, but I think in this matter they'll cooperate. They may still be angry at me over the Madrid peace talks, but it'll fade."

His quick mind in full gear, Shamir added, "I'll also convene a special cabinet meeting at seven this evening. You can brief the cabinet members before you depart for the U.S. Also invite Zvi Landau and Yaakov Cohen."

"I will."

"You know, I'm surprised the Shin Bet had not tracked the Essenes earlier."

Davidov nodded. "So am I. When this crisis is over, we can look into it further. For now, I think we need to focus on one objective—apprehend the Essenes before they can launch their attack."

"I completely agree. You have my full authority to do whatever you deem necessary to stop their treason."

Shamir's expression suddenly softened and his voice took on a philosophical tone. "I'm glad you had the good fortune to know Harry McClure. He sounds like someone I'd like to meet. Just think, without his expertise, we wouldn't have known of the Essene conspiracy until it was too late to act." Stepping from behind his desk, Shamir placed his hand on Davidov's shoulder and gazed into his eyes. "You may have saved Israel from a terrible fate."

For the first time in their hour and a half meeting, Davidov smiled. "Thank you, Mr. Prime Minister."

Shamir clinched his fist. "No, it is I who will thank you when you tell me you have arrested the Essene leaders and crushed their planned attack."

# CHAPTER 60

Moments after his meeting with the Prime Minister ended, Davidov hurried down the hall to his office and quickly organized an emergency meeting with the heads of Israel's security branches: Yaakov Cohen of the Shin Bet, Ezer Weitzman of the Mossad, and Zvi Landau, of Airport Security.

Davidov requested that the director of the Shin Bet brief the committee on the details of the Essene Brotherhood conspiracy uncovered by his agents during their search of Rabbi Katz's house. Cohen fielded a barrage of intense questioning. Then, Davidov proceeded to discuss his meeting earlier in the day with the Prime Minister. "I've been authorized by the Prime Minister to do whatever is necessary to stop the Essene Brotherhood from carrying out their planned attack."

After heated discussion, they agreed on a tentative operations plan. During Davidov's trip to the United States, Yaakov Cohen would be in charge of coordinating the group's activities. Upon his return, the heads of the security branches, joined by the Chief of the Military Staff, Lt. General Eliezer Gershon, would reconvene and finalize their plan to apprehend the leaders and members of the Essene Brotherhood.

Davidov scanned the face of each man sitting at the conference table. "The Prime Minister has requested we attend a special cabinet meeting in his office this evening at seven. I advise you to be prepared for tough questioning."

Before he closed the highly charged meeting, Davidov cautioned, "Each of you now has in your possession confidential lists of individuals who have been identified as Essene Brotherhood members. To ensure that this information is not compromised, it is imperative that you limit discussion of our planned operation to individuals you trust, and then only if necessary. Remember, the Essenes have spies in high-ranking positions within the government and the military, so be especially vigilant. If there is a leak, our plans for a preemptive strike and the future of Israel will be jeopardized."

Shortly after the meeting ended, Davidov placed a call to McClure's private number. On the second ring, a deep baritone voice greeted him. "Hello?"

"Shalom, Harry. It's Ari Davidov. I'm glad I caught you."

"Good timing. I got word an hour ago that the grand jury reviewing the evidence against Mayer Rubin is close to reaching a verdict. My source indicated an indictment and a warrant for his arrest, more than likely, will be issued before the end of the week. I hope his indictment won't compromise your preemptive plans."

"It could, Harry. I was hoping the indictment would be delayed, but having anticipated a problem, I'm leaving on a flight from Israel to Washington, D.C. at one a.m. our time.

"Our ambassador to the United States has arranged an emergency meeting with Secretary of State Baker. We're going to ask your government to help us delay announcement of the indictment. I'd like you to attend the meeting."

McClure sensed the urgency in Davidov's request. "What time is your meeting at the State Department?"

"12:30 p.m."

"Okay. I'll take an early shuttle out of La Guardia and meet you at your embassy in D.C. by 11 a.m. See you then."

After Davidov hung up the phone, he pondered the ramifications of the crisis he faced. He poured and downed a shot of vodka, and for several minutes thought of his long professional and personal relationship with McClure. Gazing out of his office window at the Dome of the Rock shrine, he sighed. *Thanks, Harry.*

# CHAPTER 61

The 7 p.m. emergency cabinet meeting convened by the Prime Minister to brief his cabinet ministers on the Essene conspiracy dragged on until 11:30 p.m. As Davidov had predicted, many probing questions were directed at the men responsible for Israel's internal and external security. Especially caustic was the intense questioning of the Director of the Shin Bet.

At 11:40 p.m., Davidov was driven to an Air Force base on the outskirts of Tel Aviv and whisked aboard a waiting Boeing 747-300 aircraft. The 11-hour and 30-minute flight transported him to D.C.'s National Airport. During the flight, he managed to get four hours of much-needed sleep.

Met by an Israeli Embassy chauffeur, he arrived at the Israeli Embassy, 3514 International Drive, NW, at 10:05 a.m. Following a hot shower, a change of clothing, and a light

breakfast, Davidov was ready for a sequence of critical meetings.

McClure arrived at the embassy at 10:50 a.m., passed
through a series of security checkpoints, and then entered a
special soundproof meeting room.

"Thanks for joining me on such short notice," Davidov
said as he greeted McClure with a firm handshake. "I'll fill
you in on the details later. For now, however, I want you to
know your investigation of Mayer Rubin has enabled us to
uncover a clandestine organization that plans to assassinate the
Prime Minister and overthrow the secular Israeli government."

McClure shook his head in disbelief. "Assassinate the
Prime Minister? You're kidding?"

"No Harry, it's no joke. We only have a few days to stop
them. They've scheduled their surprise attack for Sunday, July
21st. It's a holiday in Israel called Tisha B'Av. The date marks
the destruction of the first and second temples. Our preemptive plans will be compromised if indictments against
Mayer Rubin and his co-conspirators are announced before
we apprehend the Essene leaders in Israel. We must persuade
the American government to step in and delay the indictment
of Mayer Rubin and his co-conspirators.

"So that's what they've been up to. Quite—"

Before McClure finished his sentence, the door swung
open and the Israeli ambassador to the United States, Zalman
Shova, strode into the room. Davidov smiled and introduced

McClure. The ambassador gave Davidov an approving look, then shook McClure's hand. "From what Ari has told me, you have done the State of Israel a great service."

"Thank you Mr. Ambassador," McClure replied. "I'm glad I could be of assistance to your country."

The ambassador glanced at his watch. "I'd like to hear more about Mr. Rubin, but I've arranged for us to meet with the Secretary of State, James Baker, at twelve-thirty. I don't want to be late. Let's leave now and continue our discussion in the limo."

# CHAPTER 62

On Monday, July 15, 1991, at 12:30 p.m., the Israeli ambassador, Davidov, and McClure were greeted at the United States State Department by an aide to the Secretary.

"Ambassador Shova," she said in a thick Texas drawl. "The Secretary of State will see you now." Although the United States and Israel were allies, since the Gulf War tension had existed between the Bush and Shamir governments.

The ambassador smiled affably as he shook Secretary Baker's hand. Then he introduced Davidov as a special assistant to Prime Minister Shamir and McClure as a security consultant on assignment for the Israeli government.

The Secretary motioned to the leather chairs in front of his desk and said in a voice reflecting his Texan roots, "Gentlemen, please have a seat."

Turning his head, the Secretary eyed McClure. "You're an American, Mr. McClure?"

"I am, Mr. Secretary," McClure replied in a crisp voice.

"Good, that makes us even. Two Americans, two Israelis."

Everyone laughed, but the Israeli ambassador, Davidov, and McClure knew it was a subtle way for a senior official of the Bush administration to vent its frustration with the Shamir government.

The Secretary turned to the Israeli ambassador. "What can I do for you today, Mr. Ambassador?"

A shrewd diplomat, the ambassador seized the opportunity. "Mr. Secretary, If it's alright with you, I'll get right to the reason we're here today."

The Secretary nodded. "Sure, go ahead."

"We've uncovered a conspiracy which presents an imminent security threat to Israel."

Raising his eyebrows, the Secretary asked, "What kind of threat, Mr. Ambassador?"

"I'd like Mr. Davidov to elaborate."

The Secretary turned his eyes to Davidov. "Please proceed, Mr. Davidov."

Davidov knew he had a short window to convey the gravity of the peril facing the Israeli government. In a concise narrative, he described how Israeli intelligence, aided by McClure, uncovered a conspiracy planning the destruction of the Holy Muslim Shrines on the Temple Mount in Jerusalem. "The group, Mr. Secretary, calling itself the Essene Brotherhood, is also planning to assassinate Prime Minister Shamir and blame his death on Muslim terrorists."

Noting the Secretary's jaw had tightened, Davidov continued, "A member of the conspirator group, a key fundraiser in the United States, is expected to be indicted by a grand jury convening in Brooklyn federal court. Announcement of his indictment could seriously impair our preemptive plan to apprehend all of the conspiracy leaders in Israel."

His hands clasped together, the Secretary eyed the Israeli ambassador. "This is indeed a grave situation. Any damage to Muslim buildings on the Temple Mount could ignite a new war in the Middle East and seriously sidetrack our peace initiatives in the region. How can I help you, Mr. Ambassador?"

Sensing Davidov's narrative had hit the mark, the ambassador replied, "On behalf of my government, I request your assistance in arranging a meeting with Attorney General Richard Thornburgh. We would like him to request that Judge James Rosenthal temporarily postpone the impending indictments of Mayer Rubin and his co-conspirators."

"I fully understand, Mr. Ambassador. When would you like to meet with the Attorney General?"

"If it's possible . . . today."

The Secretary recoiled. "Today? That's a tall order." For a moment, he reflected. *God, these Israelis are tough.* "Let's see what I can do. In the interim, if you don't mind, please make yourself comfortable in the lounge outside my office."

The ambassador smiled graciously. "Thank you Mr. Secretary. We'll wait."

Twenty-five minutes later, the Secretary's aide approached the Israeli ambassador's party. "Gentlemen, the Secretary would like you to join him in his office."

Addressing the ambassador, the Secretary gestured with his open hand. "I have good news. The Attorney General will see you at four-fifteen this afternoon."

The ambassador smiled. Rising to his feet, he approached Secretary Baker's desk. "Thank you, Mr. Secretary. We greatly appreciate your assistance. If we can ever reciprocate, don't hesitate to ask."

The Secretary grasped the ambassador's outstretched hand. "My pleasure, Mr. Ambassador. We're always interested in helping our allies. Do send my best regards to Prime Minister Shamir."

"I will relay your message, Mr. Secretary."

# CHAPTER 63

The stately facade of the Justice Department building, located on a trapezoidal lot at 950 Pennsylvania Avenue NW, offers few clues as to the impressive collection of Art Deco painting and statues within its cavernous interior. Surprisingly, for a federal government building, the collection also includes above a second floor doorway—a stylized portrait of Jesus Christ.

From 1935 until 1941, talented New Deal artists painted 68 murals depicting American historical scenes and symbolic interpretations relating to the role of justice in America.

During the same period, sculptor C. Paul Jennewein, who also served as overall design consultant, created 57 masterful sculptural elements. Though credited with designing the many Art Deco light fixtures throughout the interior and exterior of the building, he's best known for his 12.5-foot aluminum statue of the Spirit of Justice.

The ambassador's party entered the Justice Department on Constitution Avenue. As they passed through the Great Hall, the ambassador stopped abruptly in front of a cast aluminum Art Deco statue. He studied the statue depicting a woman wearing a toga-like dress with one breast revealed, then turned to his Justice Department escort. "I thought in America justice is blind?"

The escort smiled. "It is, but the Spirit of Justice, commissioned during the depression, is a symbolical interpretation of the unbiased role of American justice."

The ambassador was about to ask another question when Davidov interrupted. "We don't want to keep the Attorney General waiting."

The ambassador nodded. "Let's go."

The warm reception accorded the Israeli ambassador by the Justice Department attested to the power wielded by the Secretary of State within the Bush administration. With an engaging smile, the Attorney General greeted the ambassador in a stately conference room furnished with high backed leather upholstered chairs.

Soon after his guests were seated and coffee was served, the Attorney General recounted meeting Prime Minister Shamir several years earlier at a White House conference on international terrorism. Seamlessly, he then turned the discussion to the current Israeli crisis.

"Earlier today, Mr. Ambassador, acting on a call I received from Secretary Baker, I contacted the Unites States Attorney for the Southern District of New York and requested that he arrange a meeting with Federal Judge James Rosenthal. Understanding the potential ramifications of the crisis confronting your government, he assured me he would do his utmost to persuade Judge Rosenthal to temporarily postpone announcement of indictments against Mayer Rubin and the other co-conspirators."

The ambassador smiled. "My government greatly appreciates your assistance."

The Attorney General glanced at Davidov and McClure, then turned to the ambassador. "I trust my call to you tomorrow will be to confirm Judge Rosenthal has granted the Justice Department's request."

As they exited on Constitution Avenue, the ambassador grasped Davidov's upper arm. "I think the meeting went well."

"Yes, I think so. Now we have to hope Judge Rosenthal grants our request."

The ambassador smiled. "I think he will. I'll be in touch as soon I have word from the Justice Department. The ambassador glanced at his watch, then said, "I've got a meeting on Capitol Hill in about hour. Is there anything else I can help you with?"

"No. Now I need to get back to Israel."

"I understand, Ari. The limo will drop me off at the Capitol, and then it will take you and Harry to the airport."

As the limousine pulled up to the Capitol building, the ambassador turned to McClure. "We owe you a debt of gratitude, Mr. McClure. I hope the next time I see you, it will be in Israel as a guest of our government."

McClure smiled graciously and shook the ambassador's hand. "Thank you, Mr. Ambassador. I look forward to visiting Israel again."

# CHAPTER 64

As the limousine slipped into traffic on Constitution Avenue, Davidov, sitting on the back seat facing McClure, loosened his tie. "Eventful afternoon."

"I'd say," McClure replied. "I was a little concerned at the onset of our meeting with the Secretary of State. He seemed a bit testy. I got the impression he was venting some frustration with your government. But after your presentation, his attitude changed."

Davidov nodded. "You're right. Fortunately, the Prime Minister had warned me to expect some flack over his opposition to the Madrid peace talks."

"So that's what it was about."

"Yes. Now my only concern . . . will Judge Rosenthal approve the Justice Department's request?"

"He will, Ari. It's how our judicial system works. Few requests by the Justice Department, especially those related to national interests, are turned down by federal judges."

Within view of the airport, Davidov glanced at his watch. "I've got a little time. Can you join me for a drink?"

"Sure."

Choosing a table in a corner of the airport lounge, Davidov ordered a vodka tonic while McClure ordered Campari and soda.

Davidov raised his glass. "It's not over yet, but I want you to know, I appreciate everything you've done."

"I'm glad I could help you."

"When I asked you to find an M. Rubin who might be living in the U.S, I never imagined it would lead to the discovery of the Essene Brotherhood conspiracy."

"Nor did I. At least we have a chance to stop them." McClure took a sip of his drink, then asked, "Did you ever determine what the three concentric purple lines signify?"

"Yes, I meant to tell you. The purple lines on the business card we found in Kopelman's pocket are actually blue lines. My doctor wife, who's also a talented artist, helped me figure it out.

"It's a principle artists understand. When Kopelman's red blood mixed with the blue ink on the card, the blue ink turned to purple. We compared the purple lines to the three blue concentric lines on the pendant worn by one of Mayer Rubin's couriers and to the diorama found in Rabbi Katz's secret room. That's when we realized the lines represent the three walls that once surrounded Herod's Temple."

"I thought the Western Wall was the only wall that surrounded Herod's Temple?"

"No. There were two other walls on the Temple Mount the Romans destroyed when they sacked the Temple in 70 A.D. That's the reason the Essene Brotherhood adopted the three concentric blue lines as their symbol."

"And the murder of Uzi Kopelman . . . is there a link to the Essenes?"

Davidov gave a pained smile. "We found a file in Rabbi Katz's secret room documenting how they murdered him. You were right, Harry. They paralyzed him with curare, and then stabbed him to make it look like he'd been attacked by Muslim terrorists."

"I don't understand. Why did they want to kill him?"

"You may recall, I mentioned he was on his way to meet me when he was attacked."

"Yes, I remember."

"We think several days before he was murdered, Kopelman discovered that Mayer Rubin periodically wire transferred large sums of U.S. currency to accounts controlled by Rabbi Katz."

"But how would the Essenes know of Kopelman's discovery?"

"For many years, the Essenes systematically planted members throughout the government and the military. We think an Essene member, working in the Finance Ministry, informed Rabbi Katz. Fearing their conspiracy would be uncovered, Rabbi Katz gave the order to kill Kopelman."

McClure pulled a blue folder from his attaché case and handed it to Davidov. "This is an update on the data we've gathered on Mayer Rubin and his co-conspirators. It also includes additional information on Mark Federman."

Sipping his drink, McClure watched as Davidov scanned the file. When Davidov finished, he laid down the file.

"Nice work. Since we now know that Mark Federman has played a major role in the Essenes' international financial dealings, this material is timely."

McClure set his glass down and gazed at Davidov. "I understand Jews killing Muslims in defense of their country, but after all the horror of the Holocaust, a Jew killing another Jew . . . it doesn't make sense."

Davidov stared introspectively at the half-filled glass in his hand. Feeling the cool moisture on the glass against his skin, he raised his eyes and focused on McClure.

"I'll try to explain. A good analogy is what is going on in the Muslim world. Muslims don't all share the same beliefs. Many moderates have learned to live peacefully in Israel. Others are militant and believe Allah has empowered them to kill all Jews. In a similar way, many Jews in Israel practice their faith in moderation, or not at all. In contrast, fanatical right-wing Jewish groups believe Israel should exist as a religious state based on the law of the Torah. To these groups you are considered a Jew only if you strictly adhere to their unbending orthodox beliefs. Otherwise, in their eyes, you are no better than a Christian or a Muslim . . . perhaps less."

McClure listened attentively as Davidov went on.

"In 1948, when Israel was fighting for its independence, Orthodox Jewish groups, especially those in the Hasidic community in the U.S., opposed Israel's independence. They bitterly condemned the establishment of the State of Israel as sacrilegious. Israel, they argued, can only be established when the Messiah appears. Many of these groups have toned down their rhetoric, but in Israel there is a small powerful minority still believing, in preparation for the coming of the Messiah, the Temple should be rebuilt on the Temple Mount and all Muslims driven out of Israeli land."

McClure leaned forward and placed his folded hands on the table. "Can you stop them?"

"I think we can, but keep in mind—the tactics employed by the Essenes are strikingly similar to the tactics of many other religious terrorist groups. It's an ongoing struggle that's simmered for centuries. The major differences this time—the Essenes are immersed in our institutions, heavily armed, and many are Israeli citizens."

Davidov reached for his glass and finished his drink. Setting the glass down, he gazed at McClure. "I'll have to go soon, but there's something else I want you to know." Davidov paused and eyed McClure. "Are you familiar with the Weizmann Institute?"

"Sure. It's your leading scientific research and technology development center."

Davidov nodded. "Do you also know that they've developed all of our secret weapons—including a nuclear bomb?"

McClure smiled. "Yes, I've known that for some time. Is there a problem?"

"There could be. The Essenes have infiltrated the Weizmann Institute at the highest levels. If they succeed at seizing the government and Israel is then attacked by neighboring Muslim countries . . . they intend to retaliate with a nuclear device."

McClure shot back, "That could be the beginning of the end of civilization."

"Exactly. So, if we don't stop them, the Essenes may end up starting World War Three and—" Before Davidov could finish his sentence, a female aide approached him.

"The plane is ready for boarding."

Davidov nodded. "Okay. I'll be along in a minute."

Davidov stood and grasped McClure's hand. "Can we end this madness before it's too late? I hope so. Thanks, my friend. I'll be in touch."

# CHAPTER 65

A head of schedule, Davidov's plane taxied off the main runway of Ben Gurion International Airport and parked in front of a government gate. Minutes later, he thanked the crew and exited down a mobile staircase.

Escorted by a soldier armed with an Uzi submachine gun, he walked 200 feet to a waiting black Mercedes. As the limousine got underway, the chauffeur handed him a sealed envelope marked Confidential-Deliver to Ariel Davidov. The dossier, prepared by the Director of the Shin Bet, contained updates on the secret plan to apprehend the leaders and members of the Essene Brotherhood. *The Essene leaders identified on the lists retrieved from Rabbi Katz's home are now under 24-hour surveillance. Judging by their behavior, we are confident that they are unaware of our surveillance. In addition, we have enacted procedures to ensure that the government appears to be functioning as normal.*

The report continued. *As an added precaution, military officers suspected of involvement in the plot to assassinate the Prime Minister were issued a fake version of the Prime Minister's travel itinerary. The itinerary included pre-planned routes he would use to reach Jerusalem in the event of an emergency.*

Upon arriving at his office within the Israeli government buildings complex in Jerusalem, Davidov made a point of closely observing the behavior and mannerism of every soldier and civil servant he encountered throughout the complex. Though he didn't detect any unusual behavior, he was astutely aware that an intelligence leak was always possible.

As Davidov stepped into his office, Naomi rose from her desk and followed her boss into his office.

"Can I get you anything?" she asked, noting the preoccupied look on his face.

"Black coffee will be fine."

Throughout the afternoon, Davidov conferred via secure telephone with the heads of the Israeli intelligence services and the Army Chief of Staff. At 4 p.m., Naomi handed him a folder containing a single page fax from the Israeli ambassador to the United States, Washington, D.C.

*Shalom, Ari,*

*Mission a success! Judge Rosenthal this morning agreed to postpone the release of impending indictments against Mayer Rubin and co-defendants until advised by the Justice Department.*

   *Let me know if I can be of any further assistance.*

*Good luck,*

*Zalman Shova*


Pleased, Davidov gazed up at his assistant and smiled. "This is good news, Naomi. It buys us a little time." Before she could question him, he asked, "Is everything on schedule for tomorrow?"

"Yes," she said, nodding. "I've set up the meeting as you instructed. The heads of the intelligence service and Lieutenant General Gershon confirmed they'll be present for the ten o'clock meeting. To avoid arousing any suspicion, they will arrive at staggered times."

"Well done, Naomi. I want to spend some time with my family, so I'm going home in a few minutes. If you need me for anything, don't hesitate to call."

As he was leaving, Davidov turned his head and gazed through his office window at the gold domed shrine dominating the Jerusalem skyline. *How would the Temple Mount look without the Dome of the Rock? Can't let that happen.*

From his car cellphone, he placed a scrambled call to Prime Minister Shamir's office.

"He's in a meeting," the Prime Minister's secretary said, "but I'll interrupt him. Hold on."

A minute later Shamir was on the line. "Shalom, Ari. How did it go in Washington?"

"Quite well. I'm also pleased to report the preemptive plan is close to completion. All Essene leaders are under twenty-four hour surveillance. To guard against a security breach, we've implemented stringent communication rules."

"Have you encountered any problems?"

"No. Everything is going smoothly."

"When will the plan be finalized?"

"Tomorrow by 1 p.m."

"Then I'd like you and the heads of the military and intelligence services to brief me on your plan. Let's meet in my office tomorrow afternoon at 4."

# CHAPTER 66

On Saturday afternoon, July 20, 1991, while most of Israel's Jewish population prepared to observe Tisha B'Av, the most sacred Jewish holiday, second only to Yom Kippur, Rabbi Katz gathered key Essene Brotherhood leaders at his home in West Jerusalem. A momentous occasion, it signaled the culmination of more than 25 years of planning and the final preparation for the launch of "The Event" the next day—the ninth day of Av in the year 5751 of the Hebrew calendar.

In a corner of the prayer room, illuminated by the flickering candles of a tall, freestanding menorah, stood the imposing figure of Professor Avraham Taube. He was clad in a white robe. On the sleeves were embroidered a band of green and gold, the colors of the royal house of David.

On the podium across from Taube the menorah candles cast an ethereal glow on the high priest, Rabbi Katz. He was dressed in an elegant plaid ceremonial apron (ephod) that he wore over a white linen robe. A tall white linen hat adorned with a circular scarlet stripe covered his head, and from his chest hung a breastplate arranged in three rows containing twelve precious stones set in gold. On each stone, in Hebrew letters, were inscribed the name of one of the 12 ancient biblical tribes of Israel.

"It is fitting," the high priest said in a solemn tone, "as a sign to the people of Israel, that we have chosen to launch our sacred mission on the saddest day in Jewish history—Tisha B'Av. On Tisha B'Av, in 586 B.C.E, the Babylonians destroyed Solomon's Temple, the sanctuary of our God, and exiled the Jewish people to Babylonia. Five-hundred and fifty-six years later on the same day in 70 C.E., the Romans destroyed Herod's Temple. Once again the Jewish people were exiled and enslaved.

"Tisha B'Av also marks the anniversary of two other grievous events in Jewish History. In 1492, King Ferdinand of Spain designated Tisha B'Av as the final date for the expulsion of all Jews from Spain. And, let us not forget," he said gesturing with his outstretched hand, "World War I, which began on Tisha B'Av in 1914, signaled the beginning of a downward spiral for Jews in Europe ending in the Holocaust. Normally on this day, in preparation for fasting tomorrow, we would retreat into solitude. Instead we shall rejoice, for tomorrow shall mark the beginning of a new Israel."

Symbolically tilting his head upward, the high priest raised his outstretched arms in the direction of an imaginary heaven. The room quieted.

"Lord our God, King of the Universe, grant us the power to carry out our mission tomorrow and restore your sanctuary to the Temple Mount."

In unison, the Essene Brotherhood leaders, all clad in white robes and prayer shawls, responded, "Amen."

Turning to Colonel Fried, the high priest requested that he brief the Essene leaders on the plan of attack scheduled for the following day.

Referring to a color-coded map of Jerusalem and the surrounding area mounted on an easel, Fried traced the route the Prime Minister's car would travel on his way into Jerusalem. "At this crossing on King Saul Boulevard," he said, pointing to a red "X" on the map, "a remotely controlled bomb will be detonated. It will kill the Prime Minister and his driver."

For a long moment there was silence. Then Yossi Abramowitz asked, "What happens next?"

As Fried was about to reply, an unexpected loud knock at the front door jolted him. Formerly a Mossad agent, he instinctively wondered, *have we been compromised?* Moments later, the electric lights throughout the compound flickered, and then went out, leaving only the menorah candles to illuminate the prayer room.

Moving to a front window, Fried cautiously pulled back a heavy drape covering the window. Adjusting his eyes to the outside light, he noted several uniformed soldiers carrying automatic weapons in front of the compound. Alarmed, he shouted to the Essene leaders, "Armed soldiers have surrounded the building. Get the weapons!"

Minutes later, following another loud knock at the door, a commanding voice blared through a megaphone. "Rabbi Katz. You're surrounded. Open the door immediately. You and your men should come out with your hands raised in the air."

Terrified by the unexpected intrusion, the high priest's face contorted. "This cannot be happening . . . not today— no!"

Five minutes later, the compound's heavy front wooden door, blown off its hinges by a powerful charge, sent splintered shards of wood flying in every direction and extinguished the menorah candles. Soldiers armed with Uzi submachine guns rushed into the front room while another group of soldiers forced entry through a back door. The two groups, wearing night vision goggles, converged on the armed Essenes in the darkened prayer room.

An intense 10-minute gun battle ensued. When it ended, three Essene leaders where dead and 14 men, including Rabbi Katz and Yossi Abramowitz, critically wounded. The wounded were taken to Hadassah Hospital. Three other unhurt Essene leaders were handcuffed and led away to waiting army trucks.

Only two Essene leaders, later identified as Colonel Shlomo Fried and Professor Avraham Taube, escaped through a secret underground tunnel.

Soldiers encircled the yeshiva compound and remained on guard until the rabbi's house and adjoining compound were thoroughly searched and all Essene Brotherhood material and weapons confiscated.

While IDF Special Forces raided Rabbi Katz's compound in Jerusalem, at IDF Headquarters near Tel Aviv, Lieutenant General Eliezer Gershon, using the pretext, "Military intelligence has intercepted a plan by Hezbolla to attack Israel during the Tisha B'Av holiday," convened a special emergency meeting of high-ranking military officers. Among the group, Army Major General Dov Hertzog and Air Force Colonel Boaz Friedman, both Essene Brotherhood leaders involved in the conspiracy, were arrested as they entered the high security command center.

Concurrently, special army units arrested or killed several hundred Essene members in Jerusalem, Tel Aviv and Haifa, and destroyed two elaborate Essene weapons and supply centers in the Negev desert.

Shin Bet agents simultaneously arrested 14 government employees identified as Essene members and transported them to a high security detention center to await interrogation and trial.

Viewing the Temple Mount diorama in Rabbi Katz's secret room, Yaakov Cohen, knew he had been lucky. Thanks to an American he had never met, the Essene conspiracy had been crushed. There would be an investigation, a severe reprimand, but he would survive. Still, he wondered. How did I miss so blatant a peril to Israel's security? Breathing a deep sigh of relief, he reached for his cell phone and dialed Davidov's number.

# CHAPTER 67

At 8:15 on the evening of July 20, 1991, Davidov huddled with Prime Minister Shamir at a secret Negev desert location and waited for a call from the Director of the Shin Bet. On the first ring of his cellphone, he anxiously viewed the caller ID. Lifting his gaze, he looked at the Prime Minister. "It's Yaakov Cohen."

"Shalom, Ari. I've good news. You can tell the Prime Minister the crisis is over. We've crushed the Essene Brotherhood conspiracy."

With an affirmative nod and thumbs up, Davidov signaled the Prime Minister sitting across the table.

A broad grin covering his face, Shamir clenched his fist triumphantly.

Pressing the cellphone to his ear, Davidov asked, "Any casualties?"

"A few. The high priest, Rabbi Katz, was critically wounded. I'm not certain he'll survive."

"Are all of the other Essene leaders accounted for?"

"Yes, with the exception of Colonel Shlomo Fried and Professor Avraham Taube. We know Fried is wounded. As far as Taube, I'm sure we'll find him as well."

"Anything else I should know?"

"No. You'll have a full report in the morning."

"Excellent. I'll inform the Prime Minister. I'm sure he'll be pleased. Shalom."

Setting his cellphone down, Davidov said, "That's strange."

"What's strange," The Prime Minister asked, staring at Davidov.

"Yaakov said Professor Avraham Taube is still unaccounted for."

"And?" Shamir pressed impatiently.

"Well, I recall attending a lecture several years ago at the Shrine of the Book Museum on the history of the Essenes and the Dead Sea Scrolls. The featured speaker was Professor Avraham Taube of Hebrew University. During his presentation, he touched on the Essene practice of initiating new members in a ritual bath they referred to as spiritual resurrection. The Essenes, he said, were driven by a Messianic prophecy calling for the return of Israel to its biblical roots and restoration of the Temple."

For a moment, the Prime Minister thought. "Perhaps in Taube's presentation there was a deeper, darker message. We'll never know for sure, will we?"

# CHAPTER 68

The Prime Minister uncorked an aged bottle of Hungarian Slivovitz and half-filled two small glasses. Raising his glass, he offered a toast. Ari, I congratulate you on crushing the Essene Brotherhood conspirators. If their plans had succeeded, especially the destruction of the Muslim holy buildings on the Temple Mount, I'm sure the resulting demonstrations would have led to another war. Your fellow compatriots may never fully know or appreciate the service you have rendered to your country. So, on behalf of a grateful Prime Minister, I thank you."

Gratified, Davidov raised his glass. "Thank you, Mr. Prime Minister. L'Chayim."

Shamir set his glass down and gazed at Davidov. "Now that we've arrested the Essene leaders and ended their conspiracy, there is a bigger issue we need to consider. How do we handle release of information pertaining to the Essene conspiracy?"

Davidov's jaw tightened. "Any mention of the Essene conspiracy will surely find its way to the front pages of every newspaper in the world."

"I've read your preliminary report, Ari. It contains volatile information the tabloids would devour like hungry hounds."

"You're right. We could be facing a serious public relations nightmare. The fallout could seriously derail your plans for post Gulf War normalization of economic and political relations with Israel's Arab neighbors and Western Europe."

Grasping his chin, the Prime Minister said, "I can see the headlines. Israeli Prime Minister assassinated, government overturned, Muslim Holy sites desecrated, Ark of the Covenant looted from a Templar Chapel in Scotland. It's incredible. If I hadn't lived through this crisis, I would have thought it was a hoax." Shamir folded his hands and inhaled. "Do you think we can keep the news of the conspiracy confidential?"

His facial expression reflecting concern, Davidov pondered the Prime Minister's question. "We've been careful, but in the event of a press leak, we need to be ready with an appropriate response."

Shamir nodded. "I'm calling an emergency cabinet meeting at eleven 11 tomorrow morning. I want you to brief the cabinet members on how we handled the Essene conspiracy. It will undoubtedly be a grueling day of heated questioning and finger pointing."

# CHAPTER 69

A line of black government limousines converged on Kiryat HaMemshala, the Israeli Government office complex in West Jerusalem, at 10:30 on the morning of July 21, 1991. The Tisha B'Av holiday was normally spent with friends and family, but on this Sunday morning Prime Minister Shamir had summoned his cabinet ministers to an emergency meeting. While speculation ran high, only a few of the ministers knew the purpose of the extraordinary meeting.

Shamir waited until all of his cabinet ministers, the chief of the military staff, and the heads of the intelligence agencies were seated. Once the doors were sealed by uniformed guards, he rose to his feet. The room quieted.

"Gentlemen," Shamir said in a strong voice, "I thank you all for being here today. I know most of you would rather be at home with your families." Several of the ministers grumbled.

"I'm confident, however, once we get underway, you'll understand the gravity of why I summoned you here today. The highly sensitive matter we will be discussing is directly related to Israel's security. Our intelligence service uncovered a Jewish-led terrorist conspiracy aimed at overthrowing the current Israeli government, assassinating the Prime Minister, and destroying all Muslim holy buildings on the Temple Mount."

"Mr. Prime Minister," questioned a shocked Finance Minister. "Did I hear you correctly? A Jewish conspiracy to overthrow the government . . . assassinate you . . . and destroy all Muslim buildings on the Temple Mount?"

Standing behind a podium mounted on a rectangular wooden table, Shamir stared at the minister. "Yes—that's what I said. They are a right-wing Jewish terrorist group. We have seen such groups in Israel before, but nothing compared to the magnitude of this group. I've asked my assistant for Security Affairs, Ariel Davidov, to brief you on the details relating to the conspiracy."

Davidov acknowledged the Prime Minister with a nod and proceeded to disclose, to the astonishment of the cabinet ministers, the incredible story of how an American security consultant tipped his department off to a conspiracy led by a fanatical Messianic rabbi.

"The right-wing Orthodox Jewish terrorist group, calling themselves the Essene Brotherhood, has for more than twenty-five years patiently nurtured a plan to replace our elected secular government with an ultra-orthodox government based on the biblical law of the Torah.

"Fortunately, in a preemptive strike, we succeeded in apprehending or killing all of the Essene Brotherhood leaders, including several high ranking military officers, before they could launch their planned attack."

Following an intense grilling of Davidov, the Director of the Shin Bet, and the Commanding General of the IDF, the highly vocal and often belligerent ministers turned their attention to the issue of the Israeli government's responsibility for public disclosure.

"Our government," several ministers argued, "bears the responsibility for providing accurate information to the public without delay." Particularly vocal, the Minister of Justice said eloquently, "As the only representative democracy in the region, we have an obligation to our people and to the rest of the world to tell the truth—even when the truth may not be in our best interest."

Speaking for the opposing view, Major General Gershon, Commander of the IDF, argued forcefully, "Going public will damage the fragile relationship we maintain with our Arab neighbors and will only serve to provoke the Muslims to riot and possibly start another war."

After four hours of relentless questioning and open dissension, the Prime Minister abruptly sprang from his chair and gripped the podium. Thrusting his right hand in the air, he signaled his intention to speak. The room quieted.

"I have listened carefully to all of your questions and arguments. We are obviously far from an agreement, so as your Prime Minister, I will make the final decision in this matter."

Shamir paused for a moment to observe the faces around the room, and then said, "I believe any public announcement of the Essene Brotherhood conspiracy by the Israeli government carries the real risk of starting an immediate war with every Muslim country in the Middle East. A war, where once again our country could be the target of Scud missiles, is not in our best interest. It'll only serve to turn worldwide opinion against us. Accordingly, in regard to this matter, I have decided on the following policy."

Every eye in the room locked on the Prime Minister. "As long as no information related to the Essene conspiracy surfaces in the media, then it shall be our official policy not to reveal or comment on any information pertaining to this matter. We shall, unless the situation calls for a change in policy, maintain that the Essene Brotherhood conspiracy never occurred. The events surrounding the conspiracy shall be considered a state secret and the Essene Brotherhood files shall remain sealed for a period of fifty years."

A hushed silence filled the room. "I am, therefore, taking the unusual step of asking each of you to pledge, by solemn oath, not to reveal or discuss with any person not present today, any information related to the Essene Brotherhood conspiracy discussed today, unless I have expressly granted permission for you to do so."

Shamir slowly scanned the faces of the ministers in the room. "Do I have your solemn word? If you agree raise your right hand to signify your commitment." A few ministers muttered their displeasure, but in the end, all of the cabinet ministers agreed not to challenge the Prime Minister's authority.

"Are there any questions?" Hearing no comment, the Prime Minister thanked the ministers for attending and in a commanding voice announced, "The crisis which threatened Israel's fragile existence is now over. Let us go forward and build a better and stronger Israel for all Jews and Muslims who wish to live together in peace. I thank you for the service you have rendered to your country. Our meeting is—"

Spontaneously, before he could complete the sentence, everyone in the room rose and for several minutes applauded the Prime Minister. Taken by surprise, Shamir smiled graciously and accepted the applause as a sign of support and unity.

# CHAPTER 70

Eight days after Israeli Special Forces preemptively crushed the Essene Brotherhood conspiracy in Israel, a federal grand jury reconvened in the U.S. District Court, Brooklyn, NY, to deliberate the government's case against Mayer Rubin, Mark Federman and four other co-defendants.

In less than an hour, the jury handed-down indictments against all of the defendants. The 85-count indictment charged Mayer Rubin, Mark Federman and his co-defendants with securities fraud, wire fraud, bank fraud, money laundering, RICO crimes, and conspiracy. The list of charges against the co-defendants included:

*Unlawfully, willfully, and knowingly, directly and indirectly, by use of the means and instrumentalities of interstate commerce and of the mails, in connection with purchases and sales of securities, employing devices, schemes and artifices to defraud, making untrue statements of material facts necessary in order to make statements made, in light of the circumstances under which they were made, not misleading, and engaging in acts, practices and a course of business which would and did operate as fraud and deceit upon purchasers, in violation of Title 15, United States Code, sections 78j(b) and 78ff(a) and Rule 10b-5 of the Securities and Exchange Commission , Title 17, Code of Federal Regulations, Section 240.10b-5 (1986) . . .*

The next morning, a team of FBI agents, armed with federal arrest warrants issued by Federal Judge Rosenthal, descended on Mayer Rubin's home in Boro Park, Brooklyn and informed him of his indictment by a federal grand jury.

"There must be some mistake. I've done nothing wrong," Mayer angrily protested. Informed of his rights, he was handcuffed by two FBI agents and led to a waiting car. On the street, a small group of Hasidic men, several wearing prayer shawls, gathered in front of Mayer's home. Taunting the agents, they attempted unsuccessfully to block the exit path of the FBI vehicles.

Simultaneously, agents raided the midtown Manhattan law offices of Mark Federman.

Special Agent O'Hare approached the receptionist and flashed his credentials. "I'm here to see Mr. Federman."

Indifferent, she replied, "I'm sorry, he's not available."

Annoyed, Agent O'Hare raised the tone of his voice. "Perhaps you didn't hear me the first time. I'm an FBI agent. I

suggest you tell your boss I'm here to see him right now."
Suddenly overcome by fear, the young woman stared motionless at the FBI agent.

Undeterred, Agent O'Hare trailed by two of his men,
walked past the receptionist's desk and down a long corridor.
Stopping in front of an office marked Mark Federman, Esq.,
he knocked on the closed door and waited. Moments later the
door flew open. Standing in the doorway stood a gaunt,
somber-faced man dressed in a grey pin-striped suit.

"Mr. Federman?"

"Yes," the man answered, eyeing Agent O'Hare with dis-
dain. "Who are you and what reason do you have for barging
into my office?"

Presenting his credentials, Agent O'Hare replied, "I'm
with the FBI."

Reluctantly, Federman stepped back and motioned for the
FBI agents to enter his office. O'Hare signaled one of his
agents to close the door, and then pulled a legal document
from his briefcase and handed it to Federman.

Federman scanned the first page. His faced paled as he
noted his name listed on the federal indictment along with
Mayer Rubin and four other co-defendants. Raising his
eyebrows, he scornfully lashed out at Agent O'Hare. "This is
preposterous."

O'Hare responded with an icy stare. "Mr. Federman,
you're under arrest. A federal grand jury has indicted you and
your fellow co-conspirators."

Handcuffed and read his rights, an indignant Federman was escorted out of his office past a line of silent and stunned associates and secretaries.

Later in the day Mayer Rubin, Mark Federman, and four other co-defendants were formally charged in the United States District Court for the Eastern District of New York, Brooklyn, NY. They all pleaded not guilty. Due to the likelihood of the defendants fleeing, Judge Rosenthal set Mayer Rubin and Mark Federman's bail each at $3 million and ordered them to surrender their passports and restrict their travel to within 25 miles of New York City.

CHAPTER **71**

A month later, McClure delivered the keynote address at a high-level international corporate security and risk-management conference in Geneva, Switzerland. Upon returning to his New York office, he found an oversized envelope Velma had placed on his desk. Opening the envelope postmarked St. Maarten, he chuckled as he viewed a photograph of Max Eisen and his wife Katherine aboard a Windjammer sailing somewhere in the Caribbean. An enclosed card read.

*Hello Harry,*

*Soon after I accepted a generous offer to sell NovoMed and stay on as president, we decided a short vacation was in order. It's been a bumpy ride. Don't know how I could have done it without your unwavering support. I will fill you in on the*

*details when I get back. Dinner and champagne are*
*on me.*
*Best regards,*
*Max*

As he thought of how his friendship with Max Eisen
had led to the discovery of the Essene Brotherhood
conspiracy, he looked up to see Velma standing in front
of his desk.

"How's the world traveler?" she asked jokingly.

Still on European time, McClure stretched his arms over
his head and sighed. "The conference went well, but I'm glad
to be home. Since you routed me through London, I had an
opportunity to dine with an old MI6 friend and the next
morning catch a Virgin Atlantic flight into Newark. Before I
forget—"

Reaching for a package wrapped in Harrods's gift paper,
McClure handed it to Velma. "They fly these incredible
chocolates in fresh every day from Brussels."

Beaming, Velma spontaneously planted a kiss on
McClure's cheek. "You know, I love chocolate. Thank you."

McClure smiled. "My pleasure. We're having friends join
us at our country for the weekend, so I'd like to leave the
office early. Anything urgent?"

Velma handed McClure a large blue envelope marked
"Confidential: To Be Opened Only by Mr. Harry A.
McClure." A messenger delivered it a few minutes ago. It's
from Mr. Davidov."

Noting the absence of a postmark, McClure surmised Davidov had sent it in the diplomatic pouch via the Israeli embassy in Washington, D.C. "I've been expecting his report for some time. I'll take it with me and read it over the weekend."

# CHAPTER 72

O n Friday evening, shortly after his weekend house guests had retired for the night, McClure quietly retreated to his library, lit a cigar, and lowered into a comfortable fireside chair. Cutting the short side of the envelope he received early in the day from Ariel Davidov with a pocket knife, he removed a file marked CONFIDENTIAL - Prepared for Prime Minister Yitzhak Shamir, September 15, 1991. Davidov had attached a hand-written note to the front cover.

*Dear Harry,*

*The Prime Minister asked me to convey his gratitude for the extraordinary service you rendered to the State of Israel. If you think parts of the report read like a script from a Hollywood movie, you're not alone.*

*With much appreciation and best wishes,*

*Ari*

The 25-page document traced, from its inception in 1955, the history, recruiting techniques, and extensive financial resources of the Essene Brotherhood. The initial 10 pages, largely enhancements of information McClure had earlier received from Davidov, confirmed the high priest (Golan Kohan) of the Essene Brotherhood Rabbi Katz, wounded during the IDF assault on his Jerusalem compound, died in Hadassah Hospital 10 days later.

On page 11, McClure noted a comment Davidov had made in the right margin. Next to the statement, *the only Essene leader still unaccounted for is Professor Avraham Taube,* Davidov had penciled in "Mastermind of conspiracy?"

The report continued. *When soldiers discovered within the residence of the Essene high priest, Rabbi Jacob Katz, a trap door leading to a below ground chamber, they descended into a narrow tunnel that led to a hidden exit outside the compound. At the exit doorway, they found a white Essene Brotherhood robe embroidered with a band of green and gold on the right sleeve, the colors of the royal house of David. We think Professor Taube discarded the robe as he fled with a wounded Colonel Shlomo Fried. A search of Professor Taube's abandoned home on the outskirts of Tel Aviv by Shin Bet agents uncovered an extensive collection of books dealing with the Knights Templar, Freemasonry, Rosslyn Chapel in Scotland, and an unusual Atbash encoded document concealed in a 13th century Talmud. The deciphered document revealed that Avraham Taube's family lineage places him as a direct descendant of King Solomon. Enclosed is a copy of the translated text.*

Aggrieved by the murder of his chief Temple architect and trusted friend, Hiram Abis, great King Solomon, servant of Yahweh, called upon Abraham Taube, a son born of Esther, to join him and eight other men in establishing a secret Masonic order dedicated to perpetuating the Davidic line and protecting ancient Judaic building secrets passed down from Moses. Surviving the destruction of the Jerusalem Temple by Babylonian King Nebuchadnezzar and the forced exile to Babylonia, descendants of Abraham Taube, returned triumphantly to the land of Israel.

Once again, shortly before the Romans destroyed Herod's Temple in 70 AD, our ancestors, priests in the Temple of Yahweh and descendants of the Masonic order King Solomon created a thousand years earlier, protected the Davidic line. In league with the Essenes of Qumran, they secretly deposited sacred Judaic manuscripts, ancient Egyptian and Greek architectural geometry codes, large quantities of precious stones, gold, and a copper scroll detailing the location of the treasure hidden in vaults below the Temple Mount.

The priests fled from Jerusalem before the Romans destroyed Herod's Temple and dispersed throughout Europe and the Middle East. Most became Christians, but the Taube family settled in France and secretly passed from generation to generation their Orthodox Judaic beliefs and rituals.

As members of the secret order, which became known as Rex Deus, the head of each successive generation passed down to the his eldest son, as a symbol of the Davidic line, a gold Solomon Key ring depicting a snake entwined around a green and gold pillar. A thousand years later, in 1118 A.D., Rex Deus dispatched a small group of nine men to excavate the chambers and vaults below the Temple Mount. Calling themselves the Knights Templar, they uncovered the ancient manuscripts and treasures their Masonic ancestors had hidden below the Temple Mount as well as the lost diaries of Jesus Christ and his Nazarene Church.

For more than 200 hundred years, until the despotic French King Philip IV, in league with the Catholic Pope Clement, disbanded the order and attempted to seize all of their assets, the Knights Templar and their benefactors, Rex Deus, flourished.

Although officially disbanded by the Catholic Church, The Templars reorganized in Scotland and continued as an underground organization until, under the leadership of the Templar Knight and Rex Deus member, Sir William Sinclair, the Templars were incorporated into the resurrected Masonic order established during the reign of King Solomon.

Created by Sir William Sinclair in 1140 A.D., Rosslyn Chapel is a replica of Herod's Temple. The last great Judaic Temple, it was destroyed by the Romans in 70 A.D.

Within the interior and secret chambers of Rosslyn Chapel, surrounded by Celtic, Egyptian, Judaic, Templar and Freemason symbolism, are hidden the greatest treasures of ancient Judaism and early Christianity.

Signed: The Sons of Zadok

Commenting on the mysterious document Davidov concluded: *Historical information we've uncovered suggests Freemasonry, an outgrowth of the Knight Templar, bases its ritualistic ceremonies on the Masonic Order established by King Solomon. Although initially we believed the high priest, Rabbi Katz, was the leader of the Essene Brotherhood, new evidence suggests Professor Avraham Taube, a descendant of King Solomon and an heir to the Davidic line, as the true Essene Brotherhood leader. Since his youth, he patiently waited for the opportune time to declare his identity as the Kingly Judaic Messiah.*

"Astounding," McClure murmured aloud as he laid the document down. *I have a feeling we haven't seen the last of Professor Taube.* Recalling the photographs he'd found years earlier in the hidden Masonic room within his country house library, he sprang to his feet. Pressing the red splayed cross on the Templar Knight plaque mounted to the library wall, he waited anxiously for the concealed panel to swing open.

Inside the room, he opened an ancient wooden chest emblazoned with a Freemason symbol and retrieved a sepia-toned photograph of a young fair-haired woman. Dressed in a white wedding gown, she stood arm-in-arm with a young man in a dark suit, a distinctive Masonic sash draped over his shoulder.

McClure turned the photograph over and read the inscription. *Miss Kathryn Sinclair and Mr. Cyrus Brown on their wedding day, July 07, 1907, Rosslyn Chapel, Midlothian,*

*Scotland,* followed by a simple phrase, *Wine is strong, a king is stronger, women are stronger still, but truth conquers all.*

A chill rippled down McClure's spine.

# ABOUT THE AUTHOR

S. Eric Wachtel is a graduate of the University of Missouri. He lives with his wife and Russian Blue cat in Vermont and Washington, D.C. and is at work on the next Harry McClure thriller. Visit the author at www.sericwachtel.com.

9049167R0

Made in the USA
Lexington, KY
24 March 2011